TO LOVE

THE MCNALLY FAMILY

LAURA SCOTT

READSCAPE PUBLISHING, LLC

1

_____

Several loud thuds woke Jazzlyn McNally up from a sound sleep. For a minute, she thought the noise had been something she'd dreamed, then she heard it again. Louder. She wasn't sure, but it almost sounded as if several two-by-fours were being dropped.

What in the world?

She rolled out of bed, tugging her oversized T-shirt down over her gym shorts, and headed downstairs, wincing as one of the wooden boards creaked beneath her bare feet. What if the noise was from somewhere inside the house? She reached the bottom of the stairs, flattened herself against the wall, then gingerly peered around the corner, looking into the great room.

Casting her gaze over the main living area, the fireplace, the lighthouse oil painting over the mantle, and the antique glossy cherrywood furniture, nothing seemed out of place. But she knew she hadn't imagined the sounds, so as she made her way through her grandparents' old mansion, she picked up a claw hammer to use as a possible weapon.

Everything was fine inside the house, but when she

walked over to the French doors overlooking Lake Michigan, she noticed several boards strewn across the lawn.

Her gazebo!

Sick to her stomach, Jazz flung open the doors and stumbled outside.

No! It couldn't be! Two sections the gazebo she'd worked on for the past three days had been destroyed in one fell swoop. She stared in horror, her mind trying to comprehend what had happened. Vandals had struck. In fact, the sledgehammer they'd used was still lying in the center of the destruction.

But who would do such a thing? And why?

In the early morning light, she could see the area was deserted. Whoever had done this was long gone. Maybe in the time it took her to go through the house. It was difficult to tear her gaze away from the damaged remnants of her hard work.

She shivered in the crisp April breeze coming off the lake. Drawing a deep shuddering breath, she turned and went back inside to find her cell phone. She called the Clark County Sheriff's Department for the second time in a week.

The first incident, a broken window in the front door, had been bad enough.

But this? Destroying two sections of the gazebo she'd recently repaired? This time, the vandals had gone too far.

"Clark County Sheriff's Department," the female dispatcher answered. "How can I help you?"

"This is Jazzlyn McNally, and I need a deputy here ASAP. The vandals have used my sledgehammer to wreck my gazebo; it's lying in pieces across my lawn."

"I'll send a deputy," the dispatcher responded. The

woman didn't ask for her address; the entire town knew where the McNally Mansion was located.

"Thank you." Jazz disconnected from the call and combed her fingers through her disheveled hair, her inner fury subsiding to a dull resignation. Even if the police found who'd done this, she would still need to fix everything that had been destroyed. At this rate, her goal of opening the B&B before Memorial Day wasn't going to happen.

She gave herself a mental shake, knowing she needed to remain positive. She could do this. How much time before the deputy arrived? She figured she had ten minutes at the most, so she ran upstairs to the green room, her favorite, to change into a sweatshirt and jeans.

Five minutes later, Jazz returned to the kitchen to brew a pot of coffee. The scent helped her to relax a bit, and she poured a cup, grateful for the jolt of caffeine.

But when the deputy still hadn't arrived by the time she'd finished two cups of coffee, her anger began to simmer. By eight o'clock in the morning, she tapped her foot on the floor, wondering how long it would take for someone to arrive.

Apparently, vandalism of personal property wasn't high on the Clark County Sheriff's list of priorities.

Another hour passed. A knock at the front door made her frown. She hadn't heard a car come up the driveway. Setting her coffee aside, she reached for her claw hammer and made her way to the newly repaired front door. She peeked through the recently replaced window.

A man roughly six feet tall with longish dark hair stood there, wearing a threadbare red and gray checkered flannel shirt, faded black jeans, and construction boots.

Not the deputy.

The vandal? But why knock at her door?

She hesitated so long he rapped again, a little louder this time. The stranger hunched his shoulders and rubbed his hands together as if he were cold. No car meant he'd either walked or hitchhiked from town.

Against her better judgment, she opened the door still holding the claw hammer in clear view as she eyed him with suspicion. "Yes?"

The stranger smiled, but it didn't reach his dark eyes. "Ms. McNally? My name is Dalton O'Brien, and I was told by Stuart Sewell from the hardware store that you might be looking for some construction help. I work hard and accept cash if you're interested."

Jazz stared at him for a long moment, wondering if this guy was really brazen enough to destroy her gazebo, then come back to ask to be paid to fix it. "How did you get here?"

He looked surprised at her question. "I hitched a ride from the Pine Cone Campsite. The driver let me out on Main Street, so I walked from there."

The Pine Cone Campsite was over twenty miles from the center of town. If he was being honest, then he probably wasn't her vandal.

Still, she didn't like the timing of his arrival.

"I can provide references if needed," O'Brien went on. "I did some work on Mrs. Cromwell's bathroom a week ago."

Jazz knew Betty Cromwell. Everyone in town knew Betty, the woman was one of the biggest sources of gossip in McNally Bay. If Betty would vouch for this guy, she may be interested.

She was just about to ask for his contact information when a dark brown sedan pulled in, the words Clark County Sheriff's Department etched along the side. Finally!

Dalton O'Brien turned to watch the cop car approach,

not looking the least bit nervous as he tucked his hands into the front pockets of his jeans.

Trusting her instincts wasn't easy. Jazz had learned the hard way that she was too naïve when it came to trusting men. Yet for some reason, she didn't think the handsome stranger was the person who'd vandalized her gazebo.

Or maybe she just didn't want to believe it.

"Ma'am, I'm Deputy Garth Lewis. I understand you've had more trouble this morning?"

"Yes." Jazz opened the door wider and gestured with her hand. "Come in, both of you. I have fresh coffee if you're interested."

Both Dalton and Deputy Lewis glanced around with interest. While she loved the beautiful great room, she led the way into the kitchen and pulled two coffee mugs out of the cabinet.

"O'Brien," Deputy Lewis said with a nod. "Are you here looking for work?"

"Yes, sir." Dalton didn't say anything more, and the two men stood awkwardly in the large kitchen.

It was reassuring that the deputy knew Dalton O'Brien by name. She handed them both steaming mugs of coffee. "Cream or sugar?"

"Black is fine," Deputy Lewis said.

"For me, too," Dalton added.

"Okay then. Mr. O'Brien, why don't you have a seat for a moment while I talk to the deputy?" She crossed over to the French doors, opened them, and then stepped back so the deputy could see the vandalism for himself.

Deputy Lewis let out a low whistle. "When did this happen?"

She crossed her arms over her Michigan State sweatshirt. "The noise woke me up at six this morning. I went through the house first, so I didn't see the damage out here right away. By the time I did whoever had done this was long gone."

The deputy met her gaze. "I saw your report about the damaged front door and now this. Do you have any enemies that we need to know about?"

"None that I'm aware of." Jazz glanced at the stranger who'd come over to see the vandalism for himself. Then she turned back to the deputy. "You probably know this house belonged to my grandparents, Jerry and Joan McNally. Our family has lived here in Clark County for a hundred and fifty years, since our great-great-grandparents immigrated from Ireland. The bay was named after them."

"I'm well aware of the town history," Deputy Lewis said in a dry tone.

She gestured to the interior of the large Victorian house that she was in the process of turning into The McNallys' B&B. "My siblings and I only spent summers here, until our grandma passed away, willing the property to us. You'd know more about any possible enemies than I would."

"What's the approximate cost of the damage?" Deputy Lewis asked as he pulled out a small notepad and stubby pencil.

"Around two grand," the stranger said. "Maybe less, depending on how much of the lumber can be salvaged."

She stared at him in surprise. "That's exactly what I would have estimated," she murmured. "I guess you know your way around construction sites."

O'Brien gave a curt nod. "I do."

"Well then." Jazz let out her breath in a heavy sigh. "I guess I could use a little help, if you're willing."

The stranger nodded and took another sip of his coffee.

Jazz waited for Deputy Lewis to finish his report, which included taking pictures of the crime scene. He also bagged the sledgehammer, on the off chance he might be able to lift some fingerprints from the wooden handle. The deputy left, promising to be in touch if he had any news. Afterward, she returned to the kitchen, the stranger following like her shadow.

"You hungry?" she asked.

His eyes flared with hope. "Yes, ma'am."

"Please call me Jazz, ma'am makes me feel old. Veggie omelets okay?"

"I'm not picky," he said in a wry tone.

"Good." Jazz opened the fridge and pulled out a carton of eggs and the veggies—broccoli, onions, and mushrooms that were left over from the night before. "After breakfast, we'll get to work."

He nodded again without saying anything more.

A man of few words, she thought, his dark eyes shadowed with secrets. She told herself it didn't matter why he was hitching rides and living in a campsite. Not her business one way or the other.

Jazz only needed his assistance for the next couple of weeks, then he could be on his way. Fine with her, because she didn't need any complications in her life.

Or distractions.

IN DALTON'S OPINION, the veggie omelet Jazz had made for him was the best he'd ever tasted, but as usual, he kept his thoughts to himself.

He was only here to make a few extra bucks before moving on. His plan was to head further north, knowing that construction jobs would be plentiful there during the summer months.

The damage to the gazebo made him mad, especially the way Jazz had looked so devastated at the senseless destruction.

Ms. McNally, he sternly reminded himself. Okay, yeah, she was beautiful with her long dark brown hair tousled from sleep, and her petite, curvy figure. The way she'd answered the door holding a claw hammer had made him smile, the image still burned into his memory. Beauty aside, he had no intention of crossing the line between employer and employee.

He was a drifter. As soon as this job was finished, he'd be on his way.

Truthfully, he was happy to help. He hated the idea of a young woman living in this huge rambling house alone, while vandals went to town on her gazebo.

It wasn't right. He didn't know anything about the McNally legacy, since he'd only been in town for a couple of weeks now, but he had to agree with the deputy that the culprit must be someone holding a grudge against the family.

Which meant just about anyone in town could be considered a possible suspect.

Dalton finished his second cup of coffee, then carried his dirty dishes to the sink. "Thanks for breakfast," he said, then headed outside to see what he could salvage from the wreckage.

Not expecting to be put to work right away, Dalton had left his tool belt at the Pine Cone Campsite. He considered asking Jazz to drive him over there, then figured she probably had enough tools here for him to use.

By the time Jazz joined him, he'd picked through the

entire pile. The lumber he'd stacked together on the right side of the gazebo was good enough to be used again; the left side held the lumber split beyond repair.

"That's better than I'd hoped. This could come in closer to a thousand to repair, excluding labor."

"Agreed. If you're willing loan me tools, I'll begin construction."

"I don't have extras," Jazz said, her expression full of apology. "But you can use anything I have while I head out to buy more lumber."

"Or, if you don't mind swinging past the Pine Cone Campsite, I can pick up my tools," he offered. "We can get the lumber on the way back. With both of us working, we'll get this repaired in no time."

For the first time since he'd arrived, she broke into a wide smile. "Let's do it."

She was alarmingly stunning when she smiled, and he had to force himself to turn away. What was wrong with him? His wife Debbie and their young son, Davy, have only been gone eleven months, not even a full year. He wasn't about to try replacing them in his heart.

Not now. Not ever.

He followed Jazz through the old Victorian house to the circle drive out front. He hadn't paid much attention to the three-car garage, painted yellow with white trim to match the large house, but that's where Jazz headed.

Pushing numbers into a keypad, she stood and waited for the garage door to open. He wasn't sure why he expected to see a small compact car instead of the large bright blue Chevy pick-up truck.

"Nice," he said, his tone full of appreciation. As soon as the words left his lips, he frowned. He didn't need a truck, or any other flashy items. That was part of a life he'd left behind and had no interest in returning to. All he needed was a tent, backpack, sleeping bag, and his tools.

"Thanks." Jazz didn't seem to notice anything amiss. She waited till he was seated beside her, before heading out of the garage, closing the door with the push of a button.

The ride to the campground didn't take long. Jazz followed his directions as he told her where to find his camping spot. The red tent was right where he'd left it. He slid out of the passenger seat and went over to unzip the front flap. His backpack, camping gear, and tools were tucked inside.

He emerged a few minutes later to find Jazz standing in front of his tent, regarding it thoughtfully. He lifted his construction tool belt. "I'm ready."

She nodded absently. "Do they charge you a fee to camp here?"

"Yeah, but it's nominal. Why?"

She bit her lower lip for a moment. "How would you feel about camping outside my place instead? It's free, and I'll throw in meals."

He shouldn't have been surprised, but he was. His first instinct was to refuse, he liked her too much already. But then he remembered the vandalism.

It wasn't his problem to keep her property safe. She'd notified the cops who would probably keep a close eye on things. Then again, he knew the deputies couldn't be there all the time. And if the vandals lived in town, they could be at the old Victorian and back within an hour.

"Never mind," Jazz said hastily, as if sensing his reluctance. "It's a crazy idea."

Yeah, it was, but he nodded anyway. "I'll do it."

Her green eyes widened in surprise. "You will?"

"Yes. Although we haven't agreed on an hourly wage yet."

She named a fair sum, better than he'd hoped considering she was offering meals, too.

He took a step toward her and held out his hand. "Thank you. I'll take it."

She placed her small, yet slightly calloused hand in his, sending a sliver of awareness down his spine. He did his best to ignore it as they solemnly shook.

"It's a deal." She smiled again, stealing his breath. "I'll help you pack."

"No need, I have a system." He dropped her hand and stepped back, needing distance. He went to work dismantling his campsite with the ease of long practice.

After storing his items in the space behind the bench seat, he climbed in beside her, hoping he wasn't making a huge mistake.

2

The man was virtually a stranger, yet Jazz felt an overwhelming sense of rightness as she watched Dalton pitch his tent in the spacious area between the house and the shoreline of Lake Michigan.

She firmly believed Dalton's presence here would be enough to scare off the vandals for good, something she desperately needed. She couldn't afford more costly delays.

After purchasing the replacement lumber, her renovation account was looking rather pathetic. And she still hadn't finished all the interior work either. Bathrooms in particular were expensive to update.

The thought of tagging her siblings for more capital was depressing, so she tucked it away as something to consider, later. Right now, she would rather get the gazebo back together.

Dalton was a quiet man and a hard worker. He took on most of the heavy lifting, despite her assertion that she could manage, leaving the smaller stuff for her. By one o'clock in the afternoon, she tossed her work gloves down and swiped her forehead on her sleeve. "Lunchtime."

Dalton lifted his head and nodded. "Sounds great, I'll be ready in about ten minutes."

It was the longest sentence he'd uttered since they'd returned from the hardware store. Normally she didn't mind peace and quiet, but she couldn't help being curious about the man who'd shown up on her doorstep looking for work.

Curiosity killed the cat, she reminded herself as she headed into the kitchen. Dalton had a right to his privacy and, frankly, so did she. It wasn't as if she was anxious to reveal her inner secrets, so why would he want to? Best that they stick with simple politeness.

After washing up, she took stock of what she had in her fridge. Her grocery list hadn't included feeding a man, so she had to make due with soup and sandwiches. Grandma McNally had been a wonderful cook, but Jazz hadn't been fortunate enough to be blessed with the cooking gene. Good thing her twin, Jemma, was the one who planned to prepare the breakfasts for their little business. She hoped Dalton didn't mind plain fare. Thankfully, she'd made a pitcher of lemonade last night before going to bed, so she could offer him something to drink.

Dalton came inside but quickly ducked into the bathroom. He emerged a few minutes later, his hair damp and his hands and face shiny and smelling of soap. He'd stripped off his flannel shirt, and the black T-shirt he wore clung to his muscular chest, stretching across his broad shoulders.

Not that she had any business noticing his muscles or anything else about him.

Jazz set a plate of turkey, tomato, and Swiss cheese sandwiches in the center of the table, then gestured to the pot of soup on the stove. "Soup and sandwiches today, help yourself. And there's lemonade or water to drink, nothing else I'm afraid."

Dalton nodded and ladled the beef soup into a bowl, sniffing appreciatively. "Smells great, and I'd love a glass of lemonade."

She was ridiculously pleased. She poured two glasses for them and brought them to the table. "I'm not the cook my twin sister is, but I manage."

"You have a twin?"

"Not identical, but yes, Jemma is my twin and she is as blond as I am dark. I'm the baby of the family by three full minutes." She filled her bowl with soup and then chose a seat across from him at the small table. She smiled when he heaped his plate with two large sandwiches, glad she'd made more than she'd originally planned. "Jemma and I are blessed, or cursed, with four older brothers."

He quirked his eyebrow. "Four? Surprised you're here alone, if you have older brothers."

She laughed. "They're scattered around at the moment. Jonas is deployed in Afghanistan, and Jake is currently in Dublin. Jeremy and Jesse are busy with their own lives and careers as well."

"That's a lot of Js," he muttered.

"I know, right? Thank our grandparents, Joan and Jerry, who named my father Justin. For some crazy reason, he convinced our mom to continue the J madness." She sighed. "Doesn't matter that our brothers aren't here, Jemma and I can take care of ourselves."

"But she's not here, you're alone," he pointed out.

"Jemma and her son, Trey, will be joining me next month when school is out for the year. After our grand-mother died, she left this house to the six of us. This B and B was my and Jemma's idea; our brothers simply went along with our plan."

Dalton glanced around the oversized kitchen. "It's a nice space. Doesn't need much work."

"Not in here, no, but some of the other rooms need updating." She took a healthy bite of her sandwich, mentally reviewing everything that still needed to be done. "There are seven bedrooms upstairs, each with their own bathroom, and a master suite down here where Jemma and her son will stay. I'm using one room, which only gives us six rooms to offer to our guests. After the summer tourist season, we might be able to convert the area above the garage as an additional living space."

If they made back some of their investment, and if they were able to keep the place booked the majority of the time, and if there were no more issues with vandalism.

A lot of ifs.

"It's a huge garage," he agreed. "Should be plenty of room up there to make a cozy two-bedroom apartment with a small kitchen area and a full bath."

"That's exactly my plan," Jazz said, surprised he shared her vision. "Perfect for Jemma and Trey to have some privacy away from the guests." She didn't mind living in the master suite. After everything her twin had been through, she was glad to offer the garage space to Jemma.

But none of that would happen until after the tourist season, which hopefully would bring in decent money.

Dalton nodded and finished his two sandwiches in the time it took her to eat one. When he finished his soup, he began stacking his dishes together.

"I can't eat that third sandwich, so you should finish it off, and there's more soup, too."

He hesitated, then took the third sandwich. She filled

her bowl with more soup, and they ate in silence for several minutes.

"What's the next step after the gazebo is finished?" Dalton asked.

"Depends on the weather. I want to paint it white, then move on to updating the bedrooms. The blue room has some water damage from a leaky pipe, so two walls and part of the ceiling in that room have to be taken down to the studs." Normally she loved construction projects, but the amount of work looming before her was daunting. Especially since she kept having to fix what the vandals broke. "The bathroom in the blue room, along with the bathroom in the yellow room, need new tile and updated fixtures."

He nodded thoughtfully as he finished the third sandwich. "What's your deadline?"

"I hope to be open by Memorial Day. I have three guests booked already." She'd been afraid to book too many, in case the rooms weren't finished by then. "Jemma will be here to bake and cook for our guests, which is a good thing, since that's not my forte. Six rooms should be a nice way to kick off the tourist season."

"Good plan." He pushed his empty plate aside and then helped himself to a second bowl of soup. She found herself glad she'd included meals since Dalton looked as if he could gain a few pounds.

Had he been sick? Was that why he was living in a campsite working for cash?

After finishing his soup and lemonade, Dalton carried his dirty dishes to the sink, then headed outside without saying another word.

Standing in front of the French doors that provided an amazing view of the lake, she watched Dalton for a moment, admiring the way he dove right back into the job at hand.

His biceps bulged as he levered another two-by-four into place.

Stop it. She turned away and focused on washing the dishes. After stacking them to air dry, she headed out to join Dalton. Before she could pick up the drill, her cell phone rang. She frowned when she saw the number was listed as unknown.

It was probably spam, but on the off chance it was a potential guest, she answered. "Hello?"

"Give up, you won't succeed," a low husky voice said.

"Who is this?" she demanded, hoping the panic in her voice wasn't too noticeable. But there was no answer, the caller had already disconnected.

Dalton came over to stand beside her. "Try star sixty-nine."

With trembling fingers, she did as he'd suggested, but the call didn't go through, and there was no voice mail message either. A chill ran down her spine as she lifted her gaze to his. "Nothing."

"What did the caller say?"

"He or she, it was hard to tell, told me to give up because I won't succeed." It was freaky to have this sort of a threat so soon after her gazebo was damaged, and she couldn't help wondering if there was someone outside hiding in the bushes, watching her.

Dalton stared at her for a long moment, his gaze full of concern. "Sounds like a personal message. You better let Deputy Lewis know."

"Yeah, I will." Relieved that she wasn't staying here alone, she tightened her fingers on the phone, wracking her brain in an attempt to figure out who resented her this much and why.

If anything, she was the one who had a reason to be

upset after finding her groom-to-be kissing her bridesmaid at the rehearsal dinner. She'd called off the wedding, much to Tom's dismay, although really, what had he thought? That she'd overlook something like that?

Um, no.

But would Tom be upset enough to try to make her fail at opening the B&B? If so, for what purpose? Revenge? He was the one who'd cheated on her, not the other way around.

Besides, sneaking up to destroy her gazebo wasn't his style. The last she'd heard from Jemma, Tom Duris and Megan, her former best friend, were dating hot and heavy. Seemed as if things had worked out the way they were supposed to, the two of them were obviously perfect for each other. He was moving on with his life, and so was she.

Which meant the vandal had to be someone here in McNally Bay. Someone who'd hated her grandparents so much that they were taking that anger out on the McNally grandkids.

DALTON DIDN'T like seeing the shadow of fear darkening Jazz's eyes. Clearly, the vandal had elevated his status to become a stalker.

"Who knows your cell number?" he asked.

She wrinkled her nose. "Anyone can find it on our B and B website. I haven't gotten around to hooking up a landline yet. It's an added expense I don't need right now."

Great, that wouldn't help narrow down the list of possibilities one iota. "Call Deputy Lewis," he repeated. "And block that number."

After blocking the number, she called the Sheriff's

Department. Based on the brevity of the call, apparently there hadn't been much the Deputy had been able to offer.

"That's that." Jazz's tone sounded frazzled, but her expression was one of sheer determination. "Let's get back to work."

He nodded and returned to the section of the gazebo he was in the process of repairing. He liked physical labor, but the exertion didn't eliminate the feeling of helplessness. Good thing he'd agreed to camp on her property. In fact, he hoped the idiot would come back so he could catch him in the act.

The possibility cheered him up.

They worked in harmony for another hour. The sun grew warm on his back, causing him to sweat. He knew Jazz would let him use her shower, but he didn't have a large wardrobe to pick from. Only what he could comfortably carry on his back. He made a mental note to make a trip to the laundromat. While he was there, maybe he could ask around to see if anyone held a grudge against the McNally family.

Together they were able to repair one full panel and part of the next one. By six o'clock in the evening, Jazz stepped back, looking at their progress with a smile. "We did good work today," she said. "If the weather holds, and the vandals stay away, we'll have this finished by tomorrow."

"Yeah." A wave of satisfaction washed over him. There was nothing better than creating something out of nothing. And it was the main reason that he'd gone back to his construction roots after the devastating loss of his wife and infant son.

Just that quickly the brief sliver of happiness slipped away, leaving a gaping hole in his chest where his heart had once been.

"Something wrong?" Jazz asked.

"No." He turned away. "I need to borrow your shower if you don't mind."

"Of course. Why don't you use the shower in the master suite?"

"Thank you." He tucked the tools back into his belt, then carried it to his tent. He stored them near his backpack, then drew out fresh clothes. They were wrinkled, but he didn't care. When he emerged from the tent, Jazz was putting her own tools away.

He wanted to ask where she'd learned her construction skills but feared that would only invite prying questions into his own personal life. Questions he had no intention of answering. So, he simply waited for her to finish, then followed her inside. She pointed him to the master bathroom, then headed upstairs, presumably to her room.

The hot shower felt wonderful against his sore muscles, but he didn't linger. He towel-dried his hair, grimacing at his reflection in the mirror. He needed a haircut and a shave, not necessarily in that order. When he realized he only cared about his looks because of what Jazz might think, he turned his back and quickly changed into a clean pair of blue jeans and a brown T-shirt, then pulled a plain navy-blue sweatshirt over that. Then he took a moment to roll up his dirty clothes in a tight bundle that he could store inside his backpack.

When he emerged from the bathroom, he was greeted by the mouth-watering scent of pizza.

"I'll take those for you," Jazz said, crossing over with her hand outstretched. She was wearing fresh clothes as well, her hair damp from a recent shower. He was impressed she'd beaten him down here. "I'm doing my own laundry anyway."

He hesitated, thinking about how his plan to ask around town about who resented the McNallys. Deputy Lewis was likely doing the same thing, but he knew people often avoided saying too much to the cops. Not that they would necessarily open up to a stranger, but he thought it was worth a try.

"You're not going to make me waste water, are you?" Jazz asked impatiently. "It's no problem to add your stuff to mine."

He knew she was only doing this for his benefit, since she would obviously have more clothing than he could carry around with him. Yet allowing her to wash his things would save him time in the long run, so he nodded and handed them over. "Thank you."

"Not a problem." She took the clothes and disappeared down a set of basement stairs.

The cheese on the pizza was beginning to brown, so he glanced around for a pair of oven mitts. By the time he found them, Jazz had returned.

"I'll get it." She plucked the mitts from his hands and pulled the pizza out of the oven. "I'm sorry it's nothing more than a cheap frozen pizza. I'll head to the grocery store tomorrow."

"You won't hear me complain," he said, meaning it. A man in his position ate what was offered, never knowing when or where he'd get his next meal. "And I don't expect three meals a day, breakfast and dinner is fine. Or breakfast and lunch, whatever is easier for you."

She used a pizza slicer to cut the pie into large triangles, then pulled out two plates. When they were seated at the table, she looked him directly in the eye. "A man with your work ethic could get a job anywhere."

It wasn't a question, so he didn't answer. When he bit

into his pizza, the sauce was hot enough to burn his tongue. He took a hasty sip of his lemonade.

"So?" Jazz said, her gaze questioning.

"So, what?" He didn't like where this was going. Although he had to admit he'd expected these types of questions before now.

"Why don't you have a regular job?"

"I don't want one." He took another tentative bite of his pizza. "I like my life the way it is. Drifting from place to place. No strings."

She stared at him for a long moment. He ignored her, concentrating on his meal. She must have noticed his reluctance to talk, because she didn't ask anything more.

Dalton ate in record time, then politely excused himself.

Outside, the night air was rapidly turning cool. He stood staring at the lakeshore, enjoying the gentle sound of waves lapping against the rocks. For a fraction of a second, he considered packing up his stuff and hitting the road.

He shook off the impulse, knowing that he needed to stick around long enough to protect the place. Besides, Jazz had respected his privacy by dropping the subject, so there was no reason to run.

Hadn't he figured out by now that he couldn't run from his memories? He'd tried, but they relentlessly followed him no matter how much distance he put between himself and the side-by-side gravestones he'd left behind.

He shoved the image aside and forced himself to watch the rippling waves instead. When a sense of calmness returned, he decided to walk along the property lines, familiarizing himself with the area.

A small wooded area flanked the east side of the house, providing a natural barrier from the dwelling on the other side. The rest of the space was fairly open, though, and he could see another house to the west, about half the size as the B&B, set at about the same distance from the shore as the McNally Mansion.

He didn't see any lights indicating anyone was home. He needed to remember to ask Jazz about who lived there. Maybe the occupants didn't like the idea of having a B&B nearby.

When he'd completed his rounds, Dalton decided to move the tent so that it was hidden by the gazebo. If the vandal came from the house next door, he or she wouldn't see the tent until he was practically on top of it. When he'd finished that task, he crawled inside and removed his shoes and socks. He debated stripping off his jeans, then decided against it.

He slid into his sleeping bag and closed his eyes, hoping, praying the nightmares of his past wouldn't return. It felt like five minutes later when the sound of footsteps crunching on frost covered grass woke him up.

Bolting upright, he kicked away the sleeping bag and tugged the zipper of the tent upward.

By the time he crawled out, he only caught the barest glimpse of a shadow running away, heading directly for the house to the west of the mansion. Dalton didn't hesitate but took off after him, wincing as his bare feet found several rocks along the way.

"Stop! I'm calling the cops!" he shouted. But to no avail. The figure didn't hesitate, disappearing around the corner of the house.

Then, Dalton heard the sound of a car engine.

He didn't stop running, not even when he reached the white house, but he was too late. He searched but found nothing. No car, no evidence that anyone had been there.

The vandal had gotten away.

3

Jazz woke up to the sound of Dalton's voice shouting at someone to stop. She grabbed her phone from the bedside table where it was charging and dialed 911 while simultaneously shoving her feet into her shoes. A different dispatcher answered this time, a male, so she gave her name and told the dispatcher the vandal was back.

"I'll send a deputy," he promised in a calm tone.

"Hurry!" She didn't bother to hide her impatience as she peered out the window overlooking the lake. "He's getting away!"

"Stay inside, ma'am. A deputy will be there shortly."

There was no point to staying inside, based on the way Dalton was sprinting across her lawn toward the old Stevenson place, so she disconnected from the call and clamored downstairs to the main level.

She wasted several precious seconds unlocking the French doors. Outside, she shivered in the cold night air coming off the lake and felt bad that Dalton had to sleep out here in these temperatures.

Then again, if he'd been sleeping inside, he wouldn't have caught the vandal lurking around.

She ran toward the Stevensons', raking her gaze over the area, searching for Dalton. When she didn't see him, her heart squeezed painfully in her chest.

What if the vandal had hurt him? Killed him?

"Dalton! Where are you?" The wind seemed to diminish the sound of her voice, so she tried again, screaming his name. "DALTON!"

"Here!" A dark shadow came around the corner of the white house, and her shoulders slumped in relief when she recognized Dalton's features in the moonlight.

"Thank goodness," she said, rushing over to meet him. She instinctively put her arms around him, giving him a brief hug. He surprised her by hugging her back, before stepping away. She peered up at him. "You're not hurt, are you?"

"I'm fine." His voice was low and gruff, and she wished she could tell what he was thinking. "Unfortunately, the guy got away."

"Did you get a good look at him?"

"I only saw his back as he was running." Dalton's tone held disgust. "He was fast, but he also had a good head start in the time it took me to get out of the tent. His hair looked dark, and he was wearing dark jeans and a dark jacket. But his age? No idea. Anywhere between twenty and sixty."

None of that was particularly helpful, but she didn't point it out. At least they knew it was a man who'd done this, not a woman.

Dalton stepped around her, as if to return to her place, and she noticed his feet were pale and bare in the moonlight. "Where are your shoes?"

"In the tent." He walked gingerly, and she imagined the

sprint across the lawn had done a number on the soles of his feet. The yard wasn't well maintained, she hadn't had time to work on the lawn yet, because she'd focused her efforts on the house and the gazebo, the two main attractions for the B&B.

"A deputy should be here soon," she said, falling into step beside him.

Dalton nodded. "Good. I heard a car engine, so we know he parked at the neighbor's house before coming over here." He glanced at her. "Who lives there?"

"An older couple, last name Stevenson. They actually live in Chicago but vacation here on occasion, more in the summer than the winter. I haven't seen them since I arrived a few weeks ago."

"First names?"

She tried to remember. "Alice and Bob, I think."

"They have kids?"

She finally understood where he was going. "Yes, two sons, Rich and Mark. But they're older, probably in their late thirties early forties, with kids of their own. I can't imagine they're behind this."

Dalton shrugged but didn't answer.

"Mark is younger than Rich, but he's at least five years older than my brother Jake's thirty-three. Maybe more."

"You know what they look like?"

She grimaced. "I know what they used to look like. We spent our summer's here when we were growing up. I remember them as teenagers, but even back then, the Stevenson boys didn't want anything to do with us. We were the annoying little kids hanging around bugging them."

"I bet they really don't like the idea of a B and B being next to their vacation home."

"Why would they care?" Jazz thought Dalton was way

off track. "They're not around much anymore from what I can tell, and besides, it's not like they can't enjoy water sports and fishing on the lake regardless of who lives in our place."

"Your business could have a negative impact on their resale value," Dalton insisted.

She wasn't sure she agreed and thought for a moment about how much fun waterskiing and kayaking on the lake she'd had growing up. So many happy memories.

But now, all this vandalism was seriously messing with her aura. This was supposed to be the exciting new beginning for her and Jemma.

Headlights flashed and tires crunched on gravel at the front of the house. The deputy had gotten here faster than yesterday morning, she thought glumly, but it didn't matter now that the vandal was gone. Stifling a sigh, she cut across the lawn to the front of the mansion.

A different Deputy slid out of the car, a woman this time. She was taller than average and slender, despite the bulky uniform. Her hair was pulled away from her face in a tight bun, and she rested her hand on her weapon as Jazz and Dalton approached.

"I'm Deputy Waldorf," she announced. "I understand you've had some issues with vandalism?"

"Yes. My name is Jazzlyn McNally, and this is Dalton O'Brien. I live here and have hired Dalton to assist with renovations."

"I see." The deputy regarded Dalton suspiciously. "I don't recognize your name, where do you live?"

"Until tonight, I've been staying at the Pine Cone Campsite," Dalton said, apparently unfazed by her suspicious tone. "Ms. McNally asked me to stay on the property instead, so I pitched my tent behind the gazebo. I heard the guy approaching, but by the time I made it out of my tent, he was running away."

"Running where?" Deputy Waldorf asked.

"Toward the house located to the west of the McNally property. I chased after him, but he had a good head start. I heard the sound of a car engine, and by the time I reached the house, he was gone."

The deputy glanced at Jazz. "And you believe his story?"

"Yes. I heard him shout at the guy to stop, so I called nine one one, and when I looked out my window, I saw Dalton sprinting across the lawn toward the old Stevenson place. I met up with him at the house." She gestured toward Dalton's bare feet. "He didn't even stop to put his shoes on."

The deputy seemed to relax. "Okay, why don't you both head inside while I take a look around."

Dalton looked as if he was going to argue, but she quickly spoke up, "Sure. Come on, Dalton, let's take care of your feet."

The deputy followed them around the house to the backyard overlooking the lake. Jazz went in through the French doors, indicating Dalton should follow.

The deputy swept her flashlight over the area, taking note of Dalton's tent. Jazz hoped the deputy would find some clue the vandal might have left behind.

"Come into the kitchen," she told Dalton. "I'll fill a pan with warm water so you can soak your feet."

"I'm fine," he protested. "What time is it anyway?"

"One thirty in the morning." She decided against brewing a pot of coffee, even decaf at this hour might keep her awake. She put a towel on the floor in front of Dalton's chair, then filled a large pan with hot water. After setting the pan down, she waited for him to set his feet inside.

The bottoms of his feet were covered in scratches and

dried blood. He didn't wince as he soaked them in the water, even though she knew they had to sting.

"I'll be back," she said. She rose and went into the master bath for a washcloth, towels, and soap, along with a tiny first aid kit.

The deputy was still poking around outside. Jazz brought the supplies over, but when she knelt beside Dalton's chair, he held up his hand. "I can do it."

"You can't see the bottoms of your feet as well as I can," she protested.

He ignored her, using the soap and water to wash the dried blood away. While he did that, she rummaged around in the first aid kit looking for antibiotic ointment.

"Here, use this," she said, handing him the small tube.

"No, it will make a mess of your floors."

She rolled her eyes. "As if that matters? I don't want the cuts on your feet to get infected."

"They're fine." When she stared him down, he let out a heavy resigned sigh. "Okay, I'll put it on once I'm back inside the tent."

"I think you should sleep inside for what's left of the night." Jazz glanced up at him, her gaze serious. "For one thing, he probably won't come back now that he knows you're here, and besides, it's really cold out there. Didn't you see the frost on the grass?"

He looked surprised at her comment about the temperature. "I'm fine outside. It's not too cold."

"Please stay inside." Jazz knew she wouldn't sleep a wink if he insisted on going back out into the small cramped cold tent. "You can use the master suite for now. Full access to a bathroom is a good thing, right?"

He stared at her for a long minute. "A smaller room would work just as well."

Yes! She smiled in relief. "You've been using the master bathroom anyway, may as well use the bedroom, too. One less area for me to clean before Jemma and Trey arrive."

"Okay, but if you're going to insist I stay inside, then I have to pay for my meals."

"Don't be ridiculous. I have to eat anyway." The stubborn glint was back in his eyes, so she backed down. "Never mind, we'll discuss how to work out meals tomorrow."

He slowly nodded. A strange awareness shimmered between them, but the sensation vanished when the deputy sharply rapped on the French doors.

She handed Dalton the towel to dry his feet, then went over to let the Deputy in. "Did you find anything?"

"I'm afraid not." Deputy Waldorf glanced past Jazz to Dalton. "Any idea what kind of car you heard driving away?"

He looked thoughtful for a minute. "I would say not a small car, like a four-cylinder engine, but not a big truck either. Maybe a midsize vehicle?"

The deputy grimaced at the basic information and jotted a note. "Okay, if you remember anything else, give us a call."

"Are you going to mention this to Deputy Lewis?" Jazz asked. "He was the one who took the report on my damaged gazebo. I don't remember which deputy took the information on the broken window in my front door."

"Front door?" Dalton scowled. "When did that happen?"

"Earlier this week." She thought back. "Today's Thursday, right? Then it was Monday. A brick came smashing through the window of my front door." She shrugged. "At that point, I figured it was kids goofing around. Until the gazebo incident."

"And now, this one." The deputy looked thoughtful. She was pretty in the light with red hair and porcelain skin. Her eyes were as blue as the lake in the summertime. "I'll update

Deputy Lewis in the morning. We need to make sure all these reports are kept together."

"Thanks." Jazz felt better knowing that the first deputy she'd talked to would know the full story. Although they still didn't have a clue as to who would do something like this.

At least now maybe the cops would drive by more often.

She walked Deputy Waldorf through the main living area to let her out through the front door. Once the deputy was gone, she made sure to lock the dead bolt and then went back through the kitchen to do the same thing at the French doors.

"Let me know if you need anything," she told Dalton, who had already emptied the water from the pan and set it on the counter. "See you in the morning."

"Good night," he said, avoiding her gaze.

She left him alone, telling herself not to be hurt by his reticence. It would be smart to keep an emotional distance from the man, who, by his own admission, was nothing more than a drifter.

A nice, polite, hardworking, handsome drifter.

Enough. She kicked off her shoes and crawled back into bed. Only this time, sleep didn't come easily.

The more time she spent with Dalton, the more she wanted to know about him.

Too bad, he'd made it clear he wasn't going to share anything about his personal life. Which meant, she needed to get over it. And fast.

He wasn't likely to stick around for long.

DALTON TOSSED and turned on the overly soft mattress. Odd the way he'd become used to sleeping on the ground.

He climbed out of bed early and padded into the kitchen to make a pot of coffee. Since he knew Jazz liked it too, he didn't think she'd mind.

The clock over the stove read five minutes past six. Early considering the rude interruption in the middle of the night. He stared out at the gazebo, wondering if he should leave when the repair work was done.

He liked Jazz McNally, far more than he was comfortable with. Last night, when she'd knelt at his feet, it was all he could do not to haul her into his arms and kiss her.

Not good. He hadn't been remotely attracted to a woman since losing Debbie and Davy. And he didn't appreciate the desire twisting his gut into knots.

Nope, he didn't like any of it. Feelings were overrated. Existing from one job to the next was more than enough for him. He wasn't in the market for anything more.

If he was smart, he'd move on. Today even. Find another job in another town. Once the gazebo was repaired, she could easily paint it herself, then could focus on the inside work. Something she'd planned to do before he'd come along.

Yet, someone had shown up last night to do more damage to her gazebo. What if the guy noticed his tent was gone and came back to trash it again? Dalton hated the idea of someone intentionally setting out to hurt her. Turning the big mansion into a B&B was a nice idea. The quaint place located on the lake was bound to attract vacationers. A good business endeavor for the McNally twins.

The coffee maker beeped indicating the brew cycle had been completed. He filled a mug and took a sip, enjoying the dark roasted flavor.

He debated rifling through Jazz's fridge to find something to make for breakfast, then decided against it. For one thing, she'd already provided three decent meals, so it wouldn't hurt him to skip breakfast today. Secondly, and maybe more importantly, he didn't want to risk waking her up. After everything that had happened, Jazz deserved the opportunity to sleep in.

Decision made, he carried the mug outside. The dewy grass was cold against his bare feet, but he carefully set the coffee mug in a level spot and crawled into his tent. He dried his feet off as best as he could, then donned his socks and construction boots. Then he carried his tools outside, zipping the tent closed behind him.

He picked up the coffee mug and eyed the gazebo. There were eight sides total, open on top but with a railing midway around and slats running down from the midpoint to the bottom. There was only one panel left to fix, should be easy enough to complete before lunch.

Then he'd be on his way.

Once he polished off his coffee, he went to work. They'd already used the lumber they were able to salvage, so he carried over the new two-by-fours Jazz had purchased at the lumberyard.

He measured and marked the boards, then looked around for Jazz's circular saw. He found it inside the house, tucked in the corner of the room with the rest of her tools.

He picked it up, then nearly dropped it when he heard her voice.

"What are you doing?"

He turned to find Jazz standing in the kitchen, holding a cup of coffee. She was so pretty, his pulse jumped erratically as she slowly approached. "Working," he said, his voice emerging as a croak.

"Did you already eat something?"

"No, I didn't want to disturb you."

Her mouth tipped up in a rueful smile. "Right, because you thought I would have slept through the sound of the circular saw without a problem."

He looked down at the circular saw and shrugged with embarrassment. "Oh. Yeah. Sorry about that. I figured the sooner I get that last panel done, the better."

"Breakfast first. How does French toast sound?"

His stomach rumbled embarrassingly loud. "Um, good. I like French toast."

"Put the saw down, Dalton. We can work when we're finished eating."

He liked the way she said *we* as if they really were a team. He gave himself a mental head-slap. See? This was why he needed to move on. There is no *we*. There is only a woman trying to start her own business and a drifter.

He tightened his grip on the circular saw as if it were a lifeline. "I'll just take this outside and get my coffee cup." Without waiting for her to respond, he rested the saw against his thigh, opened the door, and sought the sanctuary of the cool spring air.

The effect was similar to that of a cold shower. He set the saw down on the floor of the gazebo and picked up the first board. No way was he going back inside to watch Jazz cook him breakfast.

He cut lumber for almost fifteen minutes before he heard the door open and Jazz's voice. "Breakfast is ready!"

Setting the cut board aside, he glanced over his shoulder. "Thanks."

She stared at him for a long moment, and he wondered if she'd guessed his intention to leave as soon as the gazebo was repaired. Even if she didn't pay him for his time, he'd gotten three, no, four solid meals out of it, so that made things even between them in his book.

He brushed off the sawdust as best he could, then grabbed his empty coffee cup before heading inside. The smell of maple syrup and butter was amazing, and he didn't understand why he was so hungry. Normally, he only bothered to eat at all to keep his strength up so he could work.

"More coffee?" Jazz held up the half-full coffee pot expectantly.

"Please." He set his cup on the table and slid into his usual seat. She filled his mug, then replaced the carafe on the burner. She picked up two plates, one stacked with six pieces of French toast, the other with three, and gave him the larger of the two.

"This is the last of the bread I'm afraid," Jazz said as she dropped into her seat. "I'll head to the grocery store if you don't mind working alone for an hour or so."

"I don't mind." Truthfully, he was glad she wouldn't be working at his side, less distracting that way. He took a bite of his French toast, wondering if an hour was enough time to finish the panel and disappear before she returned. The idea of her coming home to an empty house, to find his tent gone, gave him a hollow feeling in his gut.

No, it wouldn't be right to do that to her. The decent thing to do would be to wait until she returned and to tell her personally that he was moving on. Okay, maybe she'd be upset and ask questions, but he didn't have to answer. He was the one who'd approached her for work, not the other way around.

They ate in silence for a few minutes before she asked, "Do you know how to replace drywall?"

He tensed, eyeing her warily. "Yes, I've done drywall. Have you?"

She pursed her lips. "I've hung Sheetrock but haven't done the finishing work of taping and mudding. It would be great if you could help me with that project, since I need to replace some in the blue room, which I need fixed in order to offer it out to my guests."

He was stunned that she'd apparently read his mind. It was as if she'd known he was moving on and tried to think of a way to convince him to stay. Drywall work took a certain knack, an amateur attempt would show through even the best paint job.

"Um, I don't know . . ." He was interrupted by two sharp knocks at the front door.

"Excuse me." Jazz rose to her feet and went over to answer the door. He turned in his seat and saw the visitor was Deputy Lewis.

"Ms. McNally? I understand you had a visitor last night."

"Yes. Please, come in. Would you like some coffee?"

"No thanks." Deputy Lewis crossed into the kitchen, pinning Dalton with a stern look. "You're sure you saw some guy lurking outside?"

Dalton swallowed a lump of annoyance and rose to his feet, looking the deputy square in the eye. "Yes. I'm sure. He ran over to the Stevenson house and disappeared around the corner. Then I heard a car engine, and by the time I got there, he was gone."

Deputy Lewis looked at Jazz. "You didn't see the guy either?"

"I heard Dalton yell stop and saw him sprinting across the lawn in his bare feet." She picked up her coffee mug, cradling it in her hands. "I don't understand why you're suddenly suspicious of Dalton. You're the one who reassured me about him in the first place."

"Ms. Cromwell called the Sheriff's Department to check me out before she let me work on her bathroom," Dalton volunteered. "You know that I don't have a police record."

"Doesn't mean you didn't come here to cause trouble," Deputy Lewis grumbled. "Do you know a man by the name of Thomas Duris?"

Jazz's hand jerked, splashing hot coffee onto her hand. She let out a cry of pain and dropped it. The cup crashed to the floor, breaking into a hundred pieces and spilling coffee everywhere. Both men looked at her in surprise.

"Sorry." She looked embarrassed, yet ignored the mess. "Why are you asking about Tom?"

"I'm not asking you, Ms. McNally. I'm asking him." Deputy Lewis jerked his thumb in Dalton's direction.

"Never heard of him." Dalton didn't like the way Jazz's face had gone deathly pale. "Why? Who is he?"

There was a long, strained silence before Jazz pulled herself together. "He's no one important. Excuse me, I need a broom."

She stepped carefully around the mess, walking to the hallway closet. Dalton looked at the Deputy. "Who is he?" he repeated. "Someone who has a grudge against Jazz?"

The deputy nodded. "Yeah, maybe. Last night, Deputy Trina Waldorf did a little digging into Jazzlyn's background. Found out that nine months ago she basically left the guy at the altar, canceling their wedding the day before they were to exchange vows."

Dalton let out a low whistle. "That explains her reaction."

"Yeah." The deputy grimaced at the mess. "I wasn't able to find any ties between you and Duris, but I had to ask."

Dalton nodded, understanding the deputy had a job to do. "I didn't do it."

"Probably not, but it's up to me to investigate all possibilities." The deputy sighed. "Frankly, I'm glad you're here to keep an eye on things. We're going to call this Duris guy, ask him a few questions. See if he has an alibi for the past few days."

"Keep us posted on what you find out." Dalton was glad the deputy had a suspect, but at the same time, he wasn't happy about the fact that he'd have to stick around.

Oh sure, no one was twisting his arm, forcing him to stay. He could leave, putting pressure on the deputies to keep her safe.

Yet, if something bad happened to Jazzlyn, he knew he'd never forgive himself.

He'd stay. For now.

4

J azz managed to pull herself together long enough to begin cleaning up her mess, hoping the two men didn't notice her overreaction.

It bothered her that the deputy had poked his nose into her personal life. To add insult to injury, that he'd actually come here to question Dalton about Tom. Okay, maybe Deputy Lewis had good intentions, but he was still way off base.

Tom couldn't be the one behind the vandalism, it didn't make any sense. Grandma McNally had died six months ago, three months after Jazz had canceled their wedding. Why on earth would Tom resent her plan to open a B&B?

She and Tom had both worked in real estate. They'd met for the first time on opposite sides of a significant property transaction. She represented the seller, and Tom's client had been a physician looking for a good deal on a home worth one-point-two million. In the end, Tom had been good-natured about the way she'd gotten the best price possible for her client. Tom had asked her to lunch for the following day. She'd accepted, and four months later, he'd proposed.

Looking back, she realized now that he'd been more intrigued by the idea of combining their independent real estate businesses than sharing his life with her on a personal level. In fact, the way he'd been kissing Megan—well, suffice it to say he'd displayed a level of passion that had been missing in the way he'd kissed Jazz.

Jazz told herself that she was glad to have found out the truth before walking down the aisle. Canceling a wedding at the last minute was bad enough, but going through a messy divorce—who knew how much later—would have been far worse.

"Let me," Dalton said, breaking into her troubled thoughts and tugging the broom from her hands. "I'll take care of this."

She looked at him, realizing they were alone in the kitchen. Somehow, she'd missed the deputy leaving. With a grimace, she released her grip and moved out of his way.

There was still a piece of French toast left on her plate, but her appetite had vanished. Talking about her ex-fiancé had a way of doing that to her. They hadn't spoken since she'd thrown his engagement ring at him and walked away. He'd called several times, irritated at the amount of money they'd lost on the various venues.

She hadn't bothered to return his calls.

For a moment, she considered the low husky voice she'd heard from the unknown number. Could it have been Tom? Or Megan?

Nah. Again, it wasn't his style. Megan's either. Her friend had called several times, crying and apologizing for being attracted to Tom, begging forgiveness. Megan had no reason to sabotage Jazz's attempt to move away and start over with a new business. When Tom was irritated with her, he was always up front about it, not sneaking around in the dead of night with malicious intent.

"Did Deputy Lewis mention whether or not he'd gotten fingerprints off the sledgehammer?" she asked.

Dalton shook his head and dumped the remnants of the broken mug into the garbage can beneath the sink. He used the dish towel to wipe the floor down. "No, but I forgot to ask."

She sighed and rubbed her temple, willing her headache away. "I'm sure he would have told me if he'd found something. But I'd like to get the sledgehammer back. I may need it to break through the drywall in the blue room."

"Call him," Dalton suggested. "Then finish your breakfast."

"You can have it if you're hungry." She pushed her plate away and rose to her feet. "I'll do the dishes."

"Jazz." He stopped her with a hand on her arm, his dark brown eyes full of compassion. "Why don't you take some time for yourself? I can finish up here."

His offer was sweet, and while she appreciated his concern, it was her house, her mess, her issue. "I'm okay, thanks. Finish your breakfast and then let me know if there's anything in particular you'd like me to pick up at the grocery store."

He released her and stepped back, returning to his seat. "I'm not picky, buy what you like and I'll be fine." He dug into his meal, then flashed a rueful smile. "Although I will say I really enjoy your lemonade. If you're so inclined to buy more, I'd be grateful."

That made her laugh. "I'll make more lemonade before I leave so we're stocked up."

"Great." He looked like a little kid that caught a fly ball at a baseball game. Over lemonade, no less. It occurred to her just how different Dalton O'Brien was compared to Tom. The drifter was grateful for the smallest things, when Tom had been constantly pushing her to do more in their real estate business. He wanted her to be more aggressive and assertive than she was comfortable with. When she'd broached the idea of flipping houses, Tom had been horrified. He liked selling properties but didn't want to get his hands dirty. He flat out told her no wife of his was going to swing a hammer.

Ha! If only Tom could see her now. She'd swing a hammer all right, aiming directly for his gut. Okay, maybe not, but the image of him doubled over in shock made her smile.

She filled the sink with soapy water and began washing dishes. When Dalton finished his breakfast, and hers, he brought the empty plates over. Then he surprised her by picking up a fresh dish towel to begin drying.

"No need," she assured him. "They can sit out and air dry."

"I was thinking that we should finish up the gazebo first, then head to the grocery store," he said, ignoring her directive and drying the fry pan. "That way I can pay for half the food. It's only fair as I'm eating twice as much as you are."

"But we had a deal," she protested. "And the only reason I haven't paid you yet is because I need to stop at the ATM for cash."

"No rush, let's work on the gazebo first, looks like a storm might be brewing. Better to get the outside work finished before we run errands." He looked thoughtful for a moment. "Do you have the drywall you need for the blue room?"

"Not yet." She didn't understand why he was suddenly

jumping into her little remodeling project. After last night, she fully expected Dalton to leave as soon as the gazebo was finished. "But I haven't taken the old stuff down yet either. I also want to poke around in the attic a bit. There are some old trunks up there from my great-grandparents." She'd been anxious to explore the hidden treasures up there, but her priority had to be finishing up the work so she and Jemma could open their business.

"What about the paint for the gazebo?" He glanced outside. "No sense in painting yet today, but it would be nice to have it on hand."

She finished the last of the plates, then turned to face him. "I hope you're not doing this because you're feeling sorry for me."

He looked surprised. "I don't feel sorry for you, quite the opposite. I admire you, Jazz, especially the way you're tackling this project with enthusiasm. And you're paying me to help, remember?"

"Yeah," she agreed, regarding him doubtfully. "But somehow I get the impression that money isn't a big motivator for you."

He glanced away, staring down at the plate he was drying as if it needed his full attention. "It's not," he agreed softly. "I only need enough to live on, nothing more."

Considering he lived in a tent and didn't own a car, he must not need much. But she sensed she was treading on painful territory, so she dropped the subject.

Despite her brave words, she was secretly glad he was going to stick around for a while.

Not that she was afraid to be alone, but she liked working alongside Dalton.

More than she should.

Logically, she knew it wasn't smart to depend on a drifter.

Unfortunately, she was afraid that in her case it was already too late.

~

THE LAST SECTION of the gazebo went in without a hitch. With Jazz's help, the job was completed well before lunchtime.

He stood back, admiring their work. Finishing Mrs. Cromwell's bathroom hadn't given him this much satisfaction. He could easily see how great the structure would look when it was freshly painted. His fingers itched with the urge to begin the paint job, but the dark clouds overhead put a damper on that idea.

"Looks amazing, doesn't it?" Jazz stepped up beside him. "Just as I imagined."

Surprised, he asked, "Did you build it from scratch?"

"Not exactly. Grandpa had already framed it in, including the roof, before he got sick with cancer." Her expression turned sad. "My grandma took care of him until he died. She didn't last long after that, barely three months. I'm convinced she died of a broken heart."

A lump lodged in the back of his throat. If a person could die of a broken heart, then why wasn't he lying in a grave next to his wife and son? Frankly, he'd done his best to get there, first drowning his sorrows in a bottle of whiskey, then when that didn't work, packing only what he could carry on his back to leave town.

No way would he return to the place where his life had fallen apart.

"The frame needed to be more solid, so I added to his

initial structure but kept his same design," she went on. "Now that it's finished, I think white paint along with hanging flowering plants around the edges will be the perfect touch."

He cleared his throat, imagining it too well. "Agree."

She smiled and lightly patted his arm. "With your help, I'm sure I'll make my Memorial Day deadline without a problem."

He was far too aware of the warmth of her hand resting on his arm. Crazy, since he was still wearing the navy-blue sweatshirt.

A fat raindrop hit him on the head. Followed by another. Dark gray clouds swirled overhead. "Let's go," he said, heading for the French doors.

They didn't quite make it inside when the sky opened up dumping a deluge of rain. He used his body to protect Jazz as much as he could, but they were both fairly well soaked in the short time it took them to get inside.

"Perfect timing," Jazz said with a smile. She brushed her wet hair away from her face. "I needed a shower anyway."

He chuckled. "Me, too. Only now I need a real shower."

"Oh!" Jazz snapped her fingers. "That reminds me. I folded your clothes from yesterday and left them on top of the dryer. I'll be right back." She turned and headed down the basement stairs.

For a brief moment, he considered buying additional clothing so Jazz wouldn't have to wash his things so often. He wouldn't be able to take them with him when he left, but it still might be worth it. At least then he wouldn't be such an inconvenience to her.

Jazz returned carrying his black jeans, black T-shirt, and red and gray flannel. Tucked between the T-shirt and the jeans were his plain blue cotton boxers. Seeing them made him blush like a schoolkid.

"Thanks, I'll—um—take that shower now." He grabbed the clothes and retreated to the master bedroom, vowing to do his own laundry from now on.

An hour later, they were on their way to the hardware store. Jazz had decided to stop there first before picking up groceries.

She flew through the hardware store like a woman possessed, obviously having been there several times before. She bought paint first and then headed for the drywall section. The tape and mudding were easy enough to haul home, but the Sheetrock itself posed a dilemma.

After a brief debate with the owner, Stuart Sewell, she agreed to buy the drywall if Stuart covered it with a waterproof tarp that she'd return another day. The initial storm had passed, leaving a light drizzle behind, so Stuart had agreed with the plan.

"Where did you learn so much about construction?" Dalton asked, admittedly plagued with curiosity.

"My grandfather." Jazz's smile was sad. "I followed Grandpa around helping him work on maintaining the house, while Jemma spent time cooking with our grandmother. I told you me and my twin are complete opposites." She hesitated, then shrugged. "I hope he would be happy with the renovations I've done so far."

Her closeness to her grandparents was sweet and made him realize what he'd missed growing up. "I'm sure he would."

She nodded and led the way back outside. "Up next, groceries."

"Why not drop off the drywall and other items we bought first? In case the storm comes back."

She glanced up at the low-hanging dark clouds. "Good idea."

At the house, they worked together to stack the drywall in the empty bay of the three-car garage. She'd only purchased six sheets, based on his recommendation of what she'd need to repair the water damage, so it didn't take long. When that was finished, he quickly pulled out the paint too, figuring it was better to have everything safely locked up rather than sitting in the truck.

"Hungry?" Jazz asked when they were once again seated in the front seat of the truck.

"I shouldn't be," he answered dryly. "I feel like I've done nothing but eat since I met you."

Her smile was bright enough to light up an entire town. "Glad to hear it. Why don't we treat ourselves to a bite to eat at Daisy's Diner? It's a hot spot for the locals and has been here as long as I can remember."

He mentally counted the cash in his pocket. Should be enough for a modest lunch. No way was he going to allow her to pay for his meal. "Sounds good."

"The ATM is right across the street; I'll stop there first." It was downright uncanny the way she always seemed to know what he was thinking. "It's better to grocery shop on a full stomach, less impulse buys that way."

He nodded, wondering if Deputy Lewis had already questioned some of the locals about the vandalism. Jazz and her sister were turning the place into a B&B, but he remembered how Mrs. Cromwell had referred to the place as the McNally Mansion.

Was that how the locals thought of the place? As the McNally Mansion? With an undertone of resentment?

He winced and blocked the old memories threatening to resurface. Greed was a powerful motivator, as he well knew.

Don't go there, he warned himself. Stay focused on Jazz and the renovations she needed to get done so she could start her new business.

The diner was full, but they managed to snag a booth toward the back that was recently vacated by a young couple wearing business attire. He didn't know what businesses were in the area, mostly because he didn't much care. All he needed was construction work, and he preferred housing projects rather than large corporate building.

A harried female server came over to wipe down their table. Her name tag identified her as Ashley. "I'll be right with you," she said before hurrying off.

He reached for the menu tucked behind the condiments. It felt odd to be here like this, in a public place with a beautiful woman.

Not that this was a date or anything. Still, it might appear that way to others. The idea made him uncomfortable.

"What's good here?" he asked, trying to sound casual. "Any specials?"

"The specials are written on the white board over there." She gestured to the small square board propped on the edge of the counter. "Looks like today they're featuring Daisy's pot roast with red potatoes and mixed veggies."

He tucked the menu away. "Sounds good to me. Are you worried about this place being competition for the B&B?"

"Not at all. We only plan to offer meals for our guests. In fact, I plan to display marketing materials for the local restaurants, like this one." She replaced her menu as well, indicating she already knew what she intended to order. "There's a really nice restaurant a few miles from here with great food, too. It's located on the water and has outdoor seating so you can watch the sun set over the lake. It's called the Rustic Rooftop Inn."

"Sounds nice." Now that was a place to take a woman out on a date. Not him, but hopefully Jazz would find someone else who would treat her nice. While he didn't know exactly what had happened to cause her to call off the wedding, he could guess it had something to do with finding out something bad about the groom. She didn't seem like the type to get cold feet without a good reason.

Ashley returned and plunked two glasses of water on their table. "Are you ready to order?"

"I'll have the special," Jazz said. "And a glass of iced tea."

"Make it two," he said. "But replace the tea with lemonade."

"Easy enough. Thanks." Ashley tucked her pad away and hurried off.

"I was thinking of spaghetti for dinner," Jazz said. She sipped her water. "Even I can handle that."

"Give yourself a break. Everything you've cooked has been great," he protested.

She waved a hand. "You're easy to please. If Jemma were here, trust me, you'd definitely prefer her cooking to mine."

Looking into her bright green eyes, he couldn't imagine preferring anyone else.

Whoa, wait a minute. They were discussing food here, not people. And definitely not women.

"Spaghetti is fine." Time to change the subject. "Do you know the owner here? Daisy?"

"I've met her a few times, but she's about ten years older than I am, so I don't remember her as a kid." Her gaze turned thoughtful. "Although I think she used to hang out with Mark and Rich."

"Really?" He still believed the Stevensons were suspects in the vandalism. They had opportunity and motive.

Was it possible Daisy knew something about that?

Their food arrived quick, considering how packed it was. It tasted great, too.

When Ashley set their bill on the table, he scooped it up before Jazz could move.

"Give it to me," she protested. "I haven't gotten to the ATM yet to pay you."

"I'm not destitute. You've fed me more than enough. This meal is my treat."

She tried one more time to argue, then gave up. They made their way to the cashier where he gladly paid the bill, leaving a decent tip for their overworked server.

Outside, Jazz pulled up short when she saw an elderly man with a hunched frame coming toward them, leaning heavily on his cane. He glared directly at her, a sneer etched on his face.

"You're not welcome here, McNally. So why don't you pack up your crap and go back to Chicago where you belong?"

"What?" Jazz looked confused by the hateful attitude spewing from his mouth. "Why?"

"You know," he said in a harsh tone. He brought up one shaky hand and pointed at her. "Don't play innocent with me, missy. *You know!*"

Jazz gaped as he turned and walked into the diner.

"Who is he?" Dalton asked.

She slowly shook her head. "No idea."

"We need to talk to Deputy Lewis." Dalton watched the old man stump his way through the diner to the booth they'd vacated. "Apparently, we just found the guy holding a grudge against your family."

5

"I doubt he was the guy running across the lawn toward the Stevenson place." Jazz wasn't keen on the idea of talking to Deputy Lewis yet again. He was no doubt tired of her calling him with every little thing. "Not with that cane."

"No, but maybe he paid someone else to do it. We need to let the police know about his anger toward you." Dalton was like a dog with a bone, refusing to give up. "This is a good lead, Jazz. I'm sure the deputies must have their head-quarters close by."

She ignored his comment and walked across the street to the ATM machine. After punching in her pin number, she retrieved the cash she needed to pay Dalton. When she handed the folded bills over, he seemed reluctant to take it.

"Ready to grocery shop?" she asked, determined to shake off the negative energy swirling around her.

He tucked the cash into the front pocket of his jeans. "Are you sure you won't report that guy to Deputy Lewis?"

"For what? Being rude?" She snorted and walked around him to head back to her truck. "Not hardly."

"Aren't you curious about who he is?" Dalton persisted as he followed her. "He's obviously upset with your grandparents about something."

"Like what? He's not in their same age range," she pointed out. "Despite the cane, I bet he's closer to mid-sixties than mid-eighties. Grandpa Jerry was eighty-eight when he passed away, Grandma Joannie was eighty-five. They had my dad much later in life than most people did back then."

"Maybe he knew your parents."

She stopped abruptly and rounded to face him. "Listen, Dalton, he's old and crabby. As far as I know, that's hardly a crime. Maybe he had a crush on my mother and resents the fact that she married my father. Or maybe he simply resents the perceived McNally wealth. Most people assumed they had more money than they had because they lived in the largest house in the area located right on the shore of Lake Michigan. Either way, I'm having a hard time imagining him hiring someone to sabotage my B and B."

He looked as if he was going to argue, but she lifted a hand. "No. I'm not going to the police to report a crabby man. End of discussion. Now, do you want to go to the grocery store or not?"

Dalton glanced toward Daisy's Diner. "You go on ahead. If you don't mind swinging by to pick me up here when you're finished, that would be great. If not, I'll find my own way back."

Was he seriously going to go back inside to interrogate that old man? To what end? She threw up her hands in defeat. "Fine. I'll swing by after I get the groceries."

"Use some of this." He pulled out the money she'd just given him, but she wasn't about to take it.

She spun away without taking his cash, fueled by annoyance, and climbed in behind the wheel of her truck. Seconds later, she was on the road, heading to the grocery store.

Her temper simmered as she pushed the plastic cart up and down the aisles, picking the items she thought she'd need to provide meals over the next few days. Dalton was supposed to be helping her renovate the house, not investigate who was upset with her and why. Had he been a cop before becoming a drifter? He didn't act like a cop, not to mention he was incredibly knowledgeable about construction.

Whatever. She didn't care about Dalton's past, only his willingness to help her get the B&B into shape so that they could offer the rest of the rooms to paying guests over the upcoming tourist season. Getting the business off the ground was her priority. For her sake, and for Jemma's too.

Her twin has been through a rough time with her ex-husband and needed to get away from the area where Randal lived and worked. Jemma had been granted sole custody of their son, Trey, so she wasn't prohibited from moving. As a teacher, finishing out the school year was important to her sister, and Jazz agreed with her plan.

She made a mental note to check in with Jemma later that evening, after the school day.

Lost in her thoughts, she didn't hear anyone behind her until a cart rammed into her backside. She stumbled forward, wincing at the flash of pain.

"Oh, sorry," a female voice said in a tone that was anything but apologetic.

She whirled around to see who was behind her. It was a woman who looked to be in her fifties, wearing baggy sweatpants and a bulky sweater covering her wide frame.

"Did you hit me on purpose?" Jazz asked bluntly.

"Of course not." The woman lifted a brow as if offended and then turned to go in the opposite direction as if nothing had transpired between them.

Jazz stared after the lady for a moment, knowing full well the woman hadn't run into her by accident.

What was going on here anyway?

Did everyone in Clark County hate the McNallys? And if so, for Pete's sake, why?

DALTON STOOD inside Daisy's Diner for a moment, looking for the server who'd taken their order. When Ashley stepped past him, he lightly snagged her arm. "Excuse me, do you have a minute?"

"Not really, can't you see how busy we are?" Ashley glanced at him over her shoulder, her expression softening as she remembered him. "Oh, hi. Did you forget something?"

"No. Listen, I know you're busy, but can you tell me who that guy is sitting in the booth we just left? The one who uses a cane?"

She turned to see who he meant. "Sure. That's Leon Tate."

"Do you know why he's upset with Jazzlyn McNally?"

Ashley shrugged. "No idea. I'm new to the area myself, have only been here about a year." Her tone indicated it was already a year too long.

He noticed several customers were craning their necks, looking for her, so he dropped his hand from her arm. "Thanks, Ashley, I appreciate the information."

"Sure." She hurried back to work.

Dalton considered heading over to confront the guy but sensed it would only make things worse. Now that he had the guy's name, he headed toward Mrs. Cromwell's place. If anyone would know why Leon Tate was holding a grudge against Jazz McNally, it would be the town's biggest gossip.

The rain stopped for a moment, but the air was thick and heavy with humidity as he made his way to Mrs. Cromwell's house. When he knocked at her door, she looked surprised to see him.

"Dalton. What brings you here?"

"Hi, Mrs. Cromwell, sorry to bother you, but I'm wondering if you'd be willing to provide Jazzlyn McNally a reference on my behalf. She's looking for some construction help."

She beamed. "Of course, come on in."

He stepped inside her house and followed her into the kitchen. "Did you know the McNallys?"

"Yes, I knew them. They've been here longer than the town." She gestured for him to take a seat at the kitchen table. "Do you need me to write something out for you?"

He nodded. "If you don't mind."

"You did good work here," she said, patting his arm.

She pulled out a sheet of flowered stationery that looked a bit yellowed with age and picked up a pen. She dashed off a reference and signed her name with a flourish. "Here you go, I hope this helps you out."

"Thanks, Mrs. Cromwell, it will." He folded the note and tucked it in his pocket. "Ms. McNally has had two episodes of vandalism in the past week, do you know of anyone who might be holding a grudge against her or her family?"

"I heard about the damage to her gazebo, such a shame." Mrs. Cromwell tsk-tsked. "Unfortunately, there are several people who might hold a grudge against the McNallys, you know how it is with old wealthy families. Someone's undies are always tied up in a knot over the littlest transgression."

Mrs. Cromwell wasn't helping as much as he'd hoped. "What about Leon Tate? He told Jazz to go back to Chicago because no one wants her here."

"I guess I'm not surprised," Mrs. Cromwell admitted. "Leon attended high school with Justin McNally, and the two boys never did get along."

"Why not?" Dalton pushed. "I mean, what could be so bad that he'd be mad at Jazzlyn all these years later?"

"Nothing specific that I recall, but they were always competing with each other. Sports, jobs, cars, girls, you name it. There was a rumor that they once almost came to blows over who would get the last slice of pizza."

"Girls? Like Jazzlyn's mom?"

"Probably." Mrs. Cromwell shrugged. "I don't remember specifics, but it wouldn't surprise me if they fought over the same girl. But to be honest I don't believe Justin's wife was from the area. I think they met while she was here on vacation. Or maybe at college."

Her opinion reinforced what Jazz suspected. Yet he couldn't see why Tate would hold a grudge against Jazz because he loved her mother and couldn't have her, what, forty years ago, maybe more.

"Okay, thanks, Mrs. Cromwell." He stood and checked his watch, hoping he'd make it back to Daisy's before Jazz came looking for him. "Appreciate the reference."

"Anytime." She walked with him back to the door. "Come back and visit again soon," she called after him as he left.

He waved a hand in acknowledgment. Walking fast, he

made his way back to the diner just as Jazz pulled up in her bright blue Chevy truck.

The groceries were stored neatly behind the bench seat, making him feel guilty about the fact that she hadn't allowed him to pay his share. And that she'd done all the work herself.

"Does the name Leon Tate mean anything to you?" he asked while she drove home.

"Sounds familiar." She shrugged. "I think the Tates have been here almost as long as the McNallys."

"Mrs. Cromwell seems to think he had a thing for your mom." He filled her in on the competitive nature between Leon and Justin when they were in high school. "Your dad ever mention anything about that?"

"Not that I remember." She frowned. "He and my mom were very much in love. It was hard on all of us when they died in a freak train crash in Europe two years ago."

He inwardly winced. "I'm sorry, I didn't realize."

"It's okay." Her smile was sad. "We like to think they are up in heaven, together."

"I'm sure they are."

Once they were back at the McNally Mansion and the groceries were put away, he volunteered to begin working on the blue room.

Jazz insisted on helping. He didn't mind having a partner so much, except that her scent, rain mixed with lilacs, messed with his concentration.

He did his best to take on the heavy lifting, although the way Jazz kept glaring at him confirmed she was on to him.

Jazz brought a radio for background music.

"What are we listening to?" he asked in horror.

She cocked a brow. "Eighties tunes. My favorite."

"You weren't even born when this music hit the charts."

She shrugged. "I still prefer it over country."

"What's wrong with country?"

"Every song sounds the same. Blah, blah, blah."

He put a hand over his heart and winced. "Ouch. That hurt."

"Too bad." She flashed a cheeky smile that made him laugh.

Despite their different tastes in music, they worked in harmony for the rest of the afternoon and were covered in drywall dust by the time they'd finished cutting away all of the spots damaged by water. The gaping hole looked bad, but he knew it was really a positive sign of their progress.

"Okay, let's carry in the Sheetrock from the garage," she said, swiping her sleeve over her brow. "Once that's finished, I'll start dinner."

"Sounds good."

They made several trips between the house and the garage. The sheets of drywall were bulky but not that heavy. By the time they brought the last one in, though, he could tell she was fighting fatigue.

"We can work on hanging this new stuff tomorrow," she said, slapping the dust off her hands.

"I'll work for a bit while you make dinner," he said. "Unless you'd rather have help in the kitchen."

"I don't need help, spaghetti and meatballs isn't difficult." She shrugged. "Suit yourself. I'll let you know when it's almost ready."

There was a streak of drywall dust across her cheek that he was tempted to swipe away with his thumb. She turned and left before he could act on his impulse, which was probably a good thing.

He tried not to listen as Jazz showered in her room down

the hall before going downstairs to the kitchen. Since she wasn't there, he turned the radio to his favorite country station and worked for another forty-five minutes, hanging one full sheet and then fitting in a second one at the corner. When he finished, he stepped back and surveyed the work yet to be completed.

They'd easily finish the rest of the drywall before noon. The taping and first coat of mudding could be accomplished afterward. If the rain would hold off, they might be able to start painting the gazebo while they waited for the drywall joints to dry.

Not a bad plan, he thought with a satisfied smile. He turned, shut down the radio, and headed downstairs, where Jazz was moving around in the kitchen.

"Do I have time to shower and change?" he asked, conscious of his disheveled and sweaty appearance.

"Sure, but make it quick. Dinner will be ready in fifteen."

He didn't argue but hastened to the master suite to meet her deadline.

The mouthwatering scent of garlic bread and oregano greeted him when he returned in fourteen of his allotted fifteen minutes. "Smells great."

"Here's the salad." She thrust a large bowl of tossed greens and cherry tomatoes at him. "Plates are in the cupboard over the dishwasher."

He found the plates, silverware, and tall glasses. As promised, there was a large pitcher of lemonade in the fridge, so he filled their glasses. She pulled the garlic bread from the oven, and his stomach rumbled with anticipation, making her laugh. After cutting the bread into narrow slices, she brought the garlic bread and spaghetti and meatball sauce to the table.

"Enjoy," she said, gesturing to the food.

"After you," he insisted.

Maybe she was as hungry as he was because she didn't hesitate to fill her plate and her salad bowl. He followed suit.

They ate in silence for several long moments. One thing about physical labor, it clearly helped work up an appetite. "This is excellent," he said. "Thank you."

"You're easy to please," she teased.

"I am, but this is still amazing. Despite your lousy taste in music, you're multitalented, between doing home renovations and cooking meals."

She shrugged but looked pleased. "My music is fine. And what can I say? There's something about fixing a place up that appeals to me. I take after my grandpa that way. It's one of the reasons I initially went into the real estate business."

He thought about how he'd decided to become an architect. "Designing something beautiful from the ground up is also very rewarding."

"Designing takes a special talent." She eyed him quizzically but didn't press for more details about his past. "I can't believe how fortunate I am to have your help with this. At this rate, we'll have the other two rooms finished before Memorial Day without a problem. In fact, tomorrow morning I'm going to open the other rooms to reservations."

His gut clenched, and it was on the tip of his tongue to tell her not to depend on him to be there that long. He was already itching to move on, away from the coziness of this place.

But Jazz's green eyes were bright with anticipation, so he swallowed his instinctive protest and forced a weak smile. "I think that's a great idea."

"If we can keep all the rooms booked for the summer, we can work on the apartment over the garage." She seemed to realize what she'd said. "I mean, I'll be able to begin working on the apartment over the garage."

He didn't say anything in response, focusing on his meal. It was crazy to feel guilty over leaving the work on the garage to Jazz. She was more than capable. Sure, there was often heavy lifting that needed a second person to assist with, but that didn't need to be him.

Jazz finished eating and picked up her plate. Her cell phone rang, and she frowned as she looked at the screen. "My sister. Please excuse me." She answered the call as she walked into the living room. "Hi, Jemma, how are you?"

Unwilling to eavesdrop, he finished his last meatball and carried his dirty dishes to the sink. He filled one side of the large sink with soapy water and began washing their dishes by hand, the way Jazz had done the evening before.

The call was long, and he hoped that wasn't bad news. Jazz was still on the phone when he was done washing, so he dried the dishes too, opening cupboards until he figured out where everything belonged.

He put away the last of the silverware when Jazz returned to the kitchen, her eyes puffy and red, evidence of recent tears. He tossed the dish towel down and crossed over to meet her. "What is it? What happened?"

"Nothing," she said, her voice low and husky. He was troubled by the way she didn't meet his gaze. "Thanks for doing cleanup duty."

"Jazz." He cupped her slim shoulders in his hands, hating seeing her so upset. "You don't seem like the type to cry over nothing."

Her green eyes filled once again with tears. "I'm worried

about my sister. Her ex-husband is acting out worse than ever. I tried to talk her into bringing Trey here to McNally Bay sooner, but she's a teacher and insists on staying until the end of the school year."

"I'm sorry for what she's going through," he murmured. "Is there anything I can do?"

She shook her head. "No, and the frustrating part is that I can't do anything more either. Jemma and I are normally close, but when it comes to dealing with her ex, she pulls away from me. Makes me so mad."

"Maybe she's worried you're going to think less of her if she tells you too much."

"That would never happen," Jazz said quickly. But then she frowned. "Although now that you mention it, you could be right. I'll mention that to her the next time we talk. I appreciate your insight."

Dalton wished there was more that he could do for her and instinctively drew her into his arms, offering support.

To his surprise, she slipped her arms around his waist and pressed her cheek against his chest, holding on tight. The rain-drenched lilac scent of her teased his senses. He pressed his lips against her temple, far too conscious of how much he enjoyed cradling her close.

She clung to him for several long minutes, and frankly, he was in no rush to let her go. She fit in his arms, perfectly. Almost as if she belonged. When she finally stirred, subtly shifting from his embrace, he had to force himself to loosen his grip.

"Okay?" he asked, lifting a hand to smooth ebony strands of hair from her face.

She offered a sad smile and nodded. "Yes." She rose up and pressed a light kiss against his cheek. "Thank you."

His throat was so tight, he couldn't speak. He told himself to step away, but he couldn't tear his gaze from her mouth.

Then his desire overrode his common sense. He captured her lips with his in a gentle, soul-rocking kiss.

6

Jazz lost herself in Dalton's embrace, enjoying the gentleness of his arms around her and the way his mouth claimed possession of hers. The temptation to lean on him, soaking up his strength was strong, but something happened and he suddenly broke off the kiss and eased away.

She gulped, badly needing oxygen into her lungs, and forced herself to stand on her own two feet. She wasn't sure why he'd stopped kissing her but figured she'd done something to turn him off. How embarrassing. "I, um, should probably head upstairs."

Dalton stared at her for a long moment, and she would have given a lot to know what he was thinking. "Good night," he said in a low gravely tone. He sidestepped around her and disappeared into the master suite.

She leaned her hip against the table and lightly touched her still tingling lips. Their embrace had been all too brief, but her heart pounded erratically, and she felt as if she'd been sideswiped by a semitruck, dazed and confused.

It was her first kiss since walking away from Tom.

And she'd liked it. Very much. Probably too much, considering Dalton had made it clear he was a drifter and not sticking around for the long haul.

And even if he was going to stay for the summer, she couldn't imagine being in a relationship with a man who lived in a tent. Nothing wrong with embracing a simple lifestyle, but she was building a business here. Planning a future.

Seeking a home. And maybe, someday, a family.

She let out her breath in a heavy sigh. Okay, kissing Dalton couldn't happen again. From this point forward, he was off-limits.

After heading up to her room, she washed up and crawled into bed. But still her thoughts continued to whirl. Telling herself not to think about the guy was easy to say, but not simple to do. Just knowing they'd be working side by side the following morning, finishing up the drywall in the blue room, was enough to make her toss and turn most of the night.

The following morning, she was woken by the sound of hammering. Remembering how the vandals had hit her gazebo, she leaped out of bed and rushed into the hallway. But there wasn't a reason to continue downstairs, the pounding was coming from the blue room. And in the background was an awful country singer's twang.

She walked over to look inside. Dalton was already hard at work, replacing what looked like the last piece of Sheetrock.

"What are you doing?" she asked.

He must not have heard her approach because he spun around so fast he stumbled and nearly toppled over. "Oh, sorry." He grimaced. "I guess I woke you up."

"Nah, I sleep through hammering combined with

terrible country music all the time," she said in a deadpan tone.

Guilt flashed in his eyes. "I just wanted . . ." His voice trailed off, and suddenly she understood.

Their kiss had scared Dalton so much he wanted to finish up the work here as quickly as possible so he could move on. She supposed she should be glad he was willing to stay long enough to complete the drywall work.

"It's fine." She waved a hand dismissively. "How does scrambled eggs and bacon sound for breakfast?"

"Whatever you'd like is good with me, I'm not hungry." He turned and went back to hanging drywall.

She watched for a moment, wondering about what had put the bleak expression in his eyes. He hadn't opened up to her about his past and likely never would. None of her business, after all.

But as she turned away, she thought that his keeping his emotions bottled up inside wasn't healthy.

Thirty minutes later, she went back upstairs. "Dalton, breakfast is ready. And don't tell me you're not hungry because that won't fly with me."

He glanced at her stony expression and must have sensed he was in for a fight because he acquiesced. "Okay, thanks."

They pretty much ate in silence until she brought up the work plan for the rest of the day. "It's supposed to be sunny and nice for the next two days, so I thought I'd start painting the gazebo."

"Good idea. After I tape and mud the drywall seams, I'll come out to help."

"Great." The work was moving along faster than she'd dared to hope and all because of Dalton's help. She picked up her mug, took a sip of coffee, and eyed him over the rim.

"I want you to know how much I appreciate everything you've done for me."

"It's a job you're paying me to do," he said, dropping his gaze to the half-eaten food on his plate.

"I know, but I still appreciate it."

He lifted his gaze to hers. "As soon as I'm finished here, I'll be moving on. Making my way to Illinois or Wisconsin."

It was something she'd already known, but hearing him say the words out loud made her chest tighten with regret. "I understand."

"Do you?" He shook his head and attacked the remaining food on his plate, as if he was in a race against time, like there was some invisible clock in his head that no one else could see. When his plate was clean, he rose to his feet and then carried his dishes to the sink, disappearing from the kitchen as if the devil himself was breathing down his neck.

Jazz sat alone at the table, wrestling with the knowledge that Dalton had basically given her a warning not to place too much importance on their kiss.

She dropped her head in her hands and rubbed her temples. The stupid kiss wouldn't have happened at all if she hadn't been so upset after hearing the latest news from Jemma. The fact that Randal had actually tried to take Trey out of the K-3 preschool program was shocking. Thankfully, the teacher intervened and Randal had taken off, but still a close call.

What if he'd succeeded? Randal could have been long gone before Jemma would have known Trey was missing.

She made a mental note to call Jemma again later that afternoon, once her sister was finished with school for the day. There had to be some way to convince Jemma to come to McNally Bay sooner than later. Satisfied with that idea, she began cleaning up the breakfast dishes.

But even as she prepped for her job of painting the gazebo, she remembered the deep concern in Dalton's eyes as he rushed over to hold her when she'd finished talking to Jemma. The way he'd pulled her close and pressed a kiss along the side of her face.

No matter what he'd gone through in the past that had sent him drifting through life, in that brief moment, Dalton, a basic stranger, had shown more care and concern about what had happened to her than Tom ever had.

Truthfully? The feeling of warmth and comfort he'd shown her was something she'd secretly cherish long after Dalton was gone.

DALTON WORKED with a single-minded intensity that helped keep memories of the heated kiss he'd shared with Jazz tucked away in a small corner of his mind.

The sooner he finished the work, the faster he could leave.

He repeated the words over and over in his mind like a mantra.

Leaving now or staying longer than it would take to do the drywall work wouldn't be fair to Jazz. He was determined not to do anything that would hurt her in any way.

Which meant he needed to protect her, even from himself.

One thing about construction work, it was mindless physical labor. Good for wearing out the body, but not so great at keeping the mind preoccupied. It was a little scary how much he'd been tempted to explain to Jazz about how he'd lost Debbie and Davy, all because of the choice he'd made to put work before his family.

The knife twisting deep into his heart brought an odd sense of comfort. He should suffer for being a pathetic excuse of a husband and father. Debbie and Davy hadn't deserved to lose their lives. Especially since he could have prevented it.

If he hadn't allowed greed to get in the way.

While growing up as an only child, his parents had pushed him to be independent. He soon realized that they were anxious to get him out of the house so they could follow their dream of traveling across the globe. He was happy for them but also hadn't seen them since the funeral almost a year ago.

A sliver of guilt speared his heart, reminding him that he hadn't kept in touch with them since he'd walked away from his old life. Family had once been as important to him as it seemed to be for Jazz.

Until he'd carelessly tossed his own family away.

The walls of the house seemed to close in around him. The need to hit the road, to move on to his next job was strong.

But he'd made a promise. And this one, he wouldn't break.

When he finished mudding the joints, he cleaned up the mess, then headed outside. Jazz wasn't around, and he noticed that she'd gotten the lower part of one section painted. Realizing she had likely gone to get the ladder, he rounded the house toward the large three-car garage.

His footsteps slowed when he saw the Sheriff's Deputy vehicle sitting in the driveway. Jazz and Deputy Garth Lewis were standing and talking near the driver's side door.

He hesitated, ignoring the weird flash of jealousy that

wasn't at all welcome, debating if he should stay back to allow them privacy. But then Jazz caught his eye and gestured for him to join them, so he crossed over.

"I was just giving Ms. McNally an update on our investigation," Deputy Lewis said.

"I'm telling you, Tom isn't involved in this," Jazz insisted. "I'm sure he couldn't care less about me after all this time."

"What did you find out?" Dalton asked, pinning the deputy with a direct gaze.

"No direct evidence that he's involved, but he's in debt up to his eyeballs, and the two times I've sent a Chicago PD officer to talk to him, the guy either hasn't been home or is hiding inside avoiding the police."

Dalton narrowed his gaze. "Which means what? You haven't been able to determine if he has an alibi for the timeframe of the vandalism?"

"Exactly. We've checked, and he hasn't used any credit or debit cards in the area."

"Because he's not involved," Jazz repeated, her tone full of frustration. "It doesn't make any sense, even if he is having money trouble, why would that cause him to come out here to vandalize my property?"

"Maybe he thinks you owe him for calling off the wedding at the last minute," Deputy Lewis pointed out.

"Right." She rolled her eyes. "And vandalizing my property somehow replaces the money he lost? Besides, I paid my share of the wedding fees, we walked away fairly even on that score."

"Maybe he thinks he deserves some of your grandparents' inheritance?" Dalton glanced between Jazz and the deputy. "It's possible he thinks causing the B and B to fail means they'd have to sell the place."

"That doesn't make sense either," Jazz argued. "I asked when we learned of the inheritance, and according to my grandmother's lawyer, even if Tom and I had gotten married, the money and property of the estate would still belong to me and of course my siblings. An inheritance is not part of the Equal Marital Property Act." She sighed. "Besides, we weren't married, so he wouldn't have a claim, regardless."

Dalton still thought revenge was an angle, but then he remembered the old guy at the diner. "Leon Tate," he said.

Deputy Lewis raised a brow. "What about him?"

"You know him?" Dalton asked.

"Everyone knows him; he's as much of a fixture in this town as Mrs. Cromwell. And of course, the McNallys."

"He basically told Jazz to get out of town because no one wants her here," Dalton said. "When Jazz asked why he shook his finger in her face and said, 'You know.'"

The deputy looked surprised. "You know what?"

"I know nothing," Jazz said wearily. "The guy is old enough to be my father, how would I know why he wants me gone?"

"According to Mrs. Cromwell, Leon and Justin were both highly competitive in high school," Dalton explained. "Could be they fought over Jazz's mother or maybe some other girl."

"Or maybe people just didn't like my grandparents in general." Jazz spread her hands. "Jealousy over their imagined wealth or status . . . who knows? There are dozens of possibilities. But one thing is for sure, the old man didn't take a sledgehammer to the gazebo, run off toward the Stevensons' place, and then leap into a car to drive away."

"Not likely," Deputy Lewis agreed. "Speaking of which, I brought your sledgehammer back. We found a few usable prints but need you to come in so we can verify they're not yours."

Jazz's green eyes flashed with impatience. "I don't have time, I'm in the middle of painting the gazebo."

"You go, and I'll pick up where you left off painting," Dalton said. "It won't take long. Besides, we have the rest of the day to paint."

Jazz looked as if she wanted to argue, but Deputy Lewis jumped in. "Great idea, I'll drive you to the station and when we're finished getting your prints, I'll bring you back. Won't take long at all."

She threw up her hands in defeat. "Fine, but I need to get the ladder from the garage first. Even Dalton won't be able to reach the top of the gazebo without it."

"I'll get the ladder," he said in a firm tone. "Go with the deputy."

Jazz walked over to the garage, punched in the key code, and watched as the door raised up. "It's in the corner," she said. "And there's more painting supplies in here too, if you need them."

"I think I can handle it," he assured her.

He waited until Jazz climbed in beside the deputy and they drove off before he fetched the ladder and carried it around the house to the gazebo.

He set up the radio again, keeping it on his favorite country station. Painting was another mindless job, although he did his best to stay focused on making progress and not on what Jazz and Deputy Garth Lewis might be talking about. The fact that the deputy would be here in McNally Bay long after he was gone didn't sit well with him.

Which made no sense, since the deputy could offer Jazzlyn more on a personal level than he could.

He found himself grinding his teeth as he continued

painting. The sun was warm, so he stripped down to the thin T-shirt, making good progress on the rest of the panel. When he finished that one, he moved on to the next panel.

What in the world was taking them so long? He glanced at his watch for the third time in the past fifteen minutes. They'd been gone over an hour and a half already.

Had the Deputy taken advantage of the opportunity to take Jazz out to lunch? And why not? She was beautiful, smart, funny, handy with a hammer, down-to-earth . . .

The muffled sound of a car door slamming shut startled him from his internal monologue. His shoulders slumped in relief, and he knew in that instant that he was in trouble.

Deep trouble.

He shouldn't care this much about Jazz. About any woman. No way was he going down the road of a relationship. Not now, not ever.

With steely determination, he forced the memory of Debbie's sad expression into his mind's eye. Then he conjured up the laughing face of his son, Davy, imagining them both the last time he'd seen them, before they'd been taken from his life, forever.

He'd never have a home, or a family, again. And clearly Jazz was creating just that here in her grandparents' house.

"It's almost lunchtime, are you okay with sandwiches again?"

He turned on the ladder to glance down at Jazz. She'd turned off the radio and stood holding her hand up, shielding her eyes from the glare of the sun. He cleared his throat. "I figured you already ate."

"Why would I eat in town?" she asked, obviously confused.

He didn't want to explain his assumption that she'd gone out with the deputy, so he shrugged. "You were gone longer than I thought, figured you decided to eat before coming back."

"I waited for the deputy to verify that my prints didn't match the ones they found on the sledgehammer, and the good news is that they didn't match. We have the fingerprints of the perp who destroyed the gazebo. The bad news is that the fingerprints didn't pop up in their database."

"Bummer. Although I can't say I'm surprised. There's no reason to believe this guy has a criminal past."

"I guess not." She didn't look happy. "Give me about fifteen minutes to make the sandwiches."

"Don't forget the lemonade," he added.

She laughed before disappearing through the French doors, and he caught himself smiling in return.

Idiot. Ridiculous to be relieved that she hadn't stayed in town to have lunch with the deputy. He didn't want her to care about him. Not like that. Not when he was leaving ASAP.

He attacked the painting as if he could finish the entire section before lunchtime. Which of course, he couldn't. And while he was tempted to tell Jazz to eat without him, he knew she wouldn't let him off the hook that easily.

"Dalton! Lunch!"

"Coming," he called. He finished the last bit of trim, then climbed down the ladder. Stepping back, he surveyed their progress. Better than he'd dared hope. With both of them working the rest of the day, he saw no reason why they couldn't finish the first coat of the entire gazebo.

After cleaning off the brush and covering the paint, he headed inside. He ducked into the bathroom to quickly use the facilities and to wash up, then joined Jazz at the kitchen table.

The plate of sandwiches was heaping, and this time, instead of soup, she'd thrown together a salad.

His stomach rumbled with hunger, making a mockery out of his intent to skip lunch. Granted, the food was delicious, better than the grub he usually fixed over his campfire, but he still found it odd that he was so hungry lately.

Ever since meeting Jazz.

"Deputy Lewis doesn't believe Leon Tate is involved in the vandalism either," she said in a tone that implied she was right and he was wrong. "More likely it's kids running around getting into trouble for a cheap thrill."

"The guy I chased wasn't a kid." He was becoming annoyed at her determination to make this nothing more than a random act of violence. "The first brick through the window? Yeah, maybe. But not the guy I followed."

She wrinkled her nose in disagreement but changed the subject. "Do you think we'll get the first coat finished today?"

"Of course. We've already made significant progress. And that was with only one person doing the painting."

"Good." Her eyes glowed with excitement. "After lunch, I'm going to go on my website and make the last two rooms available as of Memorial Day."

"Why not open up sooner?" he asked between bites. "It's late April now, but the blue room walls won't take long to finish up, and that only leaves the two bathrooms to fix. Seems as if you might want to start bringing in an income sooner than later."

Her eyes widened as the idea sank in. "I could do that," she agreed. "Especially if Jemma would agree to come out here sooner."

"Exactly." He grinned and lifted his lemonade glass in a

mock toast. "To The McNallys' B and B, opening May fifteenth!"

She lifted her glass to touch the rim of his. Their gazes caught and held. Tearing his eyes from hers wasn't easy, and Dalton knew in that moment that leaving Jazz when the renovation work was complete might be one of the hardest things he'd ever have to do.

Second only to burying his wife and six-month-old son.

7

Hiding the constant sizzling awareness that she felt around Dalton wasn't easy. Especially when she suspected he felt the same way.

She tried to convince herself this was the normal camaraderie that grew between people who worked closely together, nothing more. In hindsight, she should have insisted on working on a renovation project with Tom before they got engaged. She was certain that they wouldn't have lasted an hour together without arguing, much less several days.

As if to prove her point, the rest of the afternoon passed without incident. Dalton let her pick the music for the afternoon, and she'd smiled to herself when she caught him singing along with a few of the songs. The sun was out, and the waves gently lapped against the rocky shoreline, a pleasant sound amidst the whispering wind. She and Dalton painted the gazebo in perfect harmony, a mutual system where he stayed up on the ladder leaving the lower boards and panels for her to complete.

Only when the sun began to dip on the horizon did she

remember that she needed to throw something together for dinner. She mentally reviewed the items she'd purchased at the grocery store. "Tacos sound okay to you?"

"Sure," Dalton readily agreed. "I can finish up out here if you want to get started."

"There's a lot of cleanup to do," she protested.

"I can handle it."

"That's not the point. My gazebo, my B and B, my mess."

He glanced down at her from his perch on the ladder. "Consider it repayment for all the food you're providing."

She relented, partially because he was more than capable of cleaning up, but more so because she wanted some privacy to call her twin.

Inside, she took a quick shower and used the blow-dryer to dry her hair straight. She regarded her reflection and silently chastised herself for wanting to look nice for Dalton. She ran back downstairs to the kitchen, started the ground beef browning on the stove, then called Jemma.

Her sister answered right away, as if she'd been about to call her. "Hi, Jazz."

"How are you?" Jazz asked earnestly. "Did you call the police about Randal the way I asked?"

"I did, and they took a statement from the preschool teacher. Unfortunately, the description Ms. Young gave the officer didn't match Randal, so they're not convinced my ex-husband is the one behind this."

"Ridiculous, who else would try to take Trey?" Jazz couldn't believe the cops weren't taking the threat seriously. And she was glad Jemma was finally opening up to her about the details of what was going on. "Of course, it's Randal. He must have asked someone else to pick Trey up for him."

"I tried that approach too, but they said there's no proof.

They're calling it a simple mistake." Jemma's voice was full of defeat. "You know Randal has friends on the Bloomington police force. I'm sure he has them convinced I'm crazy."

"I believe in you, Jemma, and so do a lot of other people, especially the judge who awarded you full custody of Trey," Jazz reminded her.

"For now."

Jazz didn't like the sound of that. "What do you mean?"

There was a long pause before her sister softly admitted, "I'm deeply afraid Randal will try to sue for joint custody again."

"He won't win. You have proof of his violent temper, remember?" Jazz hated knowing what her sister had suffered through before finally filing for divorce. "Hey, listen, I have an idea. The renovations here at the house are going faster than I anticipated, so why don't you give your notice now and come out in the next two weeks? I'm convinced we can rent a few rooms starting mid-May rather than waiting for the holiday weekend. But I can't do that alone, I'm not nearly the cook you are, especially when it comes to baking."

"Mid-May?" Jemma sounded skeptical. "How is that possible? You said it would take a full month to get all the work done."

She glanced out the window and watched as Dalton climbed off the ladder and began cleaning up. Muscles rippled along his back causing her pulse to jump erratically.

With an effort, she turned away and swallowed hard. "I've had a little help from a handyman," she said, hedging a bit on the truth. "Please, Jemma, take Trey and get out of Bloomington. I miss you, and you and Trey will be safer here. Not to mention, we'll be one step closer to opening our new business."

Another long pause. "I'll think about it," Jemma finally said in a low tone. "You're right about getting out of Bloomington, but I hate to leave my little second graders in the last month of school. They deserve better from me."

Jazz held the phone with one hand and jabbed a spoon into the browning meat with the other. "I know you care about your kids, Jem, but think about Trey. Is finishing the school year really worth the risk to your son?"

"No, it's not." Jemma's voice sounded brittle.

"The little ones will be fine. And so will you, once you and Trey are here with me," Jazz pressed. She set down the spoon and covered the skillet. "Please? For me? And for Trey?"

"Okay, I'll talk to the principal next week, Monday. If they can arrange for someone to cover, I'll move to McNally Bay earlier than originally planned."

Jazz performed a quick fist pump. "Great! I'll be sure to have the master suite ready for you and Trey." Remembering that Dalton was staying there, she hastily added, "But, um, give me a twenty-four-hour notice of your anticipated arrival, okay? I, uh, want to be sure I'm around and not at the hardware store or something."

"I will," Jemma promised. "Thanks, sis."

"Anytime." Jazz disconnected from the call overwhelmed with relief. There was no way Randal could know of her twin's plans, and Jazz was convinced that having Jemma here would protect her twin and her young nephew.

Since she was already on a first-name basis with Deputy Lewis, she made a mental note to let him know of Jemma's situation, just in case Randal decided to follow them here. Maybe a stranger would stand out more noticeably in a small town, compared to the large city of Bloomington, Illinois.

Dalton came into the kitchen, sniffing appreciatively. "Smells good. Do I have time for a shower?"

"Yes, I still have to cut up the tomatoes and black olives." She waved him off. "Dinner in fifteen."

He disappeared into the master suite, and she wondered if she should ask Dalton to move upstairs to the yellow room for the rest of his stay.

However long that might be.

She didn't want to think about how lonely it would feel once Dalton was gone. Oddly enough, even though he'd only been here for a few days, she'd gotten accustomed to having him around.

But he wasn't hers and he wasn't staying, so she needed to get over it. She wouldn't be alone for long anyway. Jemma and Trey would be here soon. And at some point over the next few months, each of their brothers had promised to stop by to visit. Well, except for Jonas who was deployed overseas for who knew how long.

By the end of the summer, between her family and their guests, no doubt she'd be longing for peace and quiet.

Dalton didn't say much over dinner, but she was glad to see his appetite had returned. He helped himself to a third soft shell taco heaped with guacamole. "This is great."

"Guacamole is easy." She smiled at his enthusiasm, comparing his appreciative attitude to Tom's less than agreeable countenance.

That should have been her first clue, she thought with a sigh. Not only was Tom always finding something to criticize, but he had never been satisfied with anything.

Including her, apparently, or he wouldn't have been

doing the tonsil dance with Megan after their rehearsal dinner.

Old news. No sense rehashing her failures.

"I mentioned the idea of opening earlier to my sister," she said, abruptly breaking the silence. "Jemma is going to see if she can join me sooner than originally planned."

Dalton nodded. "I'm glad to hear it."

"Yeah. Me, too."

"After dinner, I'd like you to show me the work you need done in the bathrooms," Dalton said. "Did you already buy new fixtures and tile?"

"Not yet," she admitted.

"Bring paper and pencil so I can help you make a list," he suggested. "We should be able to finish painting the gazebo tomorrow. No reason not to start in on the bathrooms."

"You still have to finish the drywall in the blue room, don't you?"

"Yeah, but this is the putzy phase, I have to wait for the paste to dry, add more, wait for that to dry, then sand it all down before we can even think of putting the first coat of spackle on. In the meantime, I can start working on other projects. Like the bathrooms. The blue room and the yellow room, right?"

She stared at him in surprise at how he had everything planned out in detail for how to proceed over the next couple of days. Logically, she knew it was only because he was determined to finish the job so he could leave town.

As if he couldn't wait to get away from her.

She forced a smile. "Right. Okay, we'll make a list."

"Good." After he carried his dishes to the sink, he disappeared upstairs to check out the bathrooms.

Bracing her hands on the sink, she stared at nothing,

wondering if there was anything she could say or do to convince Dalton to stay.

DALTON INSPECTED the bathroom in the blue room, taking note of the missing tiles and the cracked grout. Not to mention it was all the old-fashioned two-by-two size, instead of the larger ones that were more popular now.

If this place belonged to him, he'd rip all the tile out and start over fresh. It would be expensive, but he thought it would look amazing when it was finished.

Not his decision to make, especially since he had no idea what kind of a renovation budget she was working with.

Making a mental list, he moved on to the yellow room to look at that bathroom. It was in slightly better shape than the blue room, but not by much. There was no missing tile, but there may as well have been since the grout in there was seriously cracked and peeling, too.

Jazz finally joined him twenty minutes later, holding the pad and pencil in hand.

"What kind of a budget do you have?" he asked. "Tile can be pricey, and if you want me to try to salvage what's here in the yellow room, I will do my best to do that."

"I'd planned to replace the tile in here and in the blue room," Jazz said. "The green room's bathroom had been updated by my grandpa about five years ago, so it's in decent shape. The other three rooms could use updating, but they're not in horrible shape, not like these." She gestured to the tiled wall. "What are the chances there will be mold behind there once we remove everything?"

He grimaced. "Fifty-fifty. Depending on how much these

rooms have been used and the amount of moisture that may have been trapped in there."

"Right." She blew out a breath. "I guess it'll be a surprise."

A smile tugged at the corner of his mouth. He'd smiled more in the past few days than he had in the entire year. Thanks to Jazz. "I guess it will."

She made a few notes on the pad as he pointed out the various fixtures and other odds and ends that needed replacing. By the time they were finished, the way she stared at the list made him think that he'd gone overboard.

"Start with the tile, and then the tub/shower fixtures," he suggested. "The rest isn't completely necessary."

"I know." Her smile was brave. "Now that there hasn't been any more vandalism, I'm sure I'll be fine."

It was on the tip of his tongue to point out that it had been only forty-eight hours since the last attempt but decided there was no reason to play the pessimist. Instead, he edged toward the door. "I need to look at the drywall seams in the blue room, see if they're dry enough to sand down."

"Now?" she asked. "It's late; you've done enough work for the day."

He wasn't nearly as tired as he needed to be to sleep without thinking about her, so he nodded. "Yes, now. If it's dry, then I can get ahead of schedule."

"But . . ."

"I don't need any help, why don't you relax and"—he hesitated and shrugged—"I don't know, watch a movie or read a book. Whatever you normally do in your personal time."

She looked directly into his eyes, and just as last night,

he found himself leaning toward her. Somehow, he managed to catch himself before he went too far.

"But . . ."

He pulled back and rubbed the back of his neck. "Really, I don't need your help." The words came out sharper than he intended.

Jazz bit her lip, then turned and disappeared into the room near the end of the hall. She shut the door behind her with a distinct click.

He inwardly groaned, hating that he'd inadvertently hurt her feelings. He walked into the blue room, telling himself that it was better this way. She needed to stay away from him for a while.

Better for her. Better for him.

The homey feel of the place was already getting to him, making him acutely aware of what he'd never have again.

Testing the drywall plaster, he found it was still slightly moist. Not possible to sand it down until it was completely dry.

Great, just great. He whirled away from the drywall and headed back downstairs.

Unfortunately, the scent of Jazzlyn, lilacs intermixed with rain, lingered.

He couldn't believe how close he'd come to kissing her. For the second time in as many days.

And the worst thing about it was that the renovation job wasn't finished. Wouldn't be for at least four days, according to his best guess.

If there wasn't mold behind the cracked and broken tile. And if nothing else went wrong.

Call it a week. No more. Hopefully less.

Surely, he could manage to keep his hands and his mouth to himself for a measly week.

He stretched out on the bed and stared at the ceiling. Despite the physical labor he'd done, starting first thing in the morning, sleep was impossible.

After twenty minutes, he rolled off the bed and slid into his shoes. Shrugging into his flannel, he eased through the dark house and out the French doors.

He welcomed the cold spring air slapping him in the face. Moving carefully, he circled the gazebo, glad to see that it appeared undisturbed. His small red tent was right where he'd left it, possibly helping to keep intruders away by giving the impression someone was sleeping in there.

Maybe Jazz was right and the vandals were nothing but kids. Older kids. Bored young men with more testosterone than brains.

The water beckoned him and as he walked toward the lakeshore, he thought about how nice it might be to live on or near the water.

Not that he planned on settling down. Or to buy a car, or a house, or even renting an apartment. No ties at all.

No luxuries of any kind.

A glimmer of light caught the corner of his eye, and he turned and stared through the darkness sweeping his gaze along Jazz's property lines. The quarter moon was bright, but that wasn't what he'd seen.

A flashlight? Was someone out there, staking the place out to do more damage?

Then he saw it, not a flashlight, but a tiny beam of light toward the back of the old white house, the one Jazz referred to as the Stevenson place.

Someone was in there!

He sprinted across the lawn, heading straight for the house. If the Stevenson sons, Mark and Rich, were indeed living there, then he knew they had to be the ones who'd damaged the gazebo.

The house was dark on the side closest to Jazz's place, so he edged around the corner to the side that faced the lake. The light was brighter now and appeared to be in a kitchen, at least based on the edge of the cabinet he could make out through the window.

Keeping himself flat against the siding, he made his way to the window and peered inside, bracing himself to come face to face with one of the brothers.

But the room was empty.

He paused, then went back the way he came, going around to where the driveway was located.

No vehicle. He raked a gaze over the area but didn't see a garage or other out-structure.

Was there someone inside the Stevenson place? Or was the light set on a timer to make it look as if there was someone living there when there really wasn't?

He thought back to the night he'd chased the intruder. He didn't remember seeing a light in the kitchen.

But considering he'd been running to catch a vandal, it was possible he could have missed it.

Dalton turned and walked back toward the McNally Mansion. He needed to contact Deputy Lewis first thing in the morning.

They needed to understand where the Stevenson brothers were staying, once and for all.

8

Jazz woke up the next morning feeling refreshed. Her previous annoyance with Dalton had vanished, leaving a resigned acceptance in its wake.

Dalton had made it perfectly clear that he wasn't interested, so she needed to get over herself. He was a nice guy, nothing more. After all, she was paying him to work.

Speaking of which, she heard noise coming from the blue room. Not hammering this time, but he was obviously already working. The guy sure was determined to finish things up to get back on the road.

Something she should be grateful for. Without his assistance, she knew she'd never be able to open the B&B early.

She headed down the hall to look in on him. He had the door closed. She pulled it open and was greeted with a cloud of dust that made her cough. A fine sheen of white dust covered Dalton from head to toe. She was relieved to see he was wearing goggles to protect his eyes and a face mask over his nose and mouth.

He glanced over his shoulder. "Good morning." His voice was muffled by the mask. "Better stay out of here for a while."

"Okay." She coughed again and then covered her mouth with her hands. "I'm planning French toast for breakfast, if that's okay with you."

"Fine with me."

"Plan on breakfast being ready in forty-five minutes. I have some other stuff to do on the website."

He nodded, then turned back to continue with the belt sander.

Jazz made a pot of coffee, then went to work. She'd taught herself how to do the website stuff, not necessarily difficult but not intuitive either. Her experience in real estate helped. She opened up six rooms to be available starting the middle of May and then posted the same information on various social media sites, along with other B&B advertising sites.

Satisfied that she'd done as much as she could to promote their business, she stood and began making breakfast.

In exactly forty minutes, Dalton came downstairs and disappeared in the master bathroom. When he emerged, he looked amazing with his dark hair damp and long enough to curl a bit around his ears.

He helped himself to coffee while she set the platter of French toast in the center of the table.

"Do you mind if I borrow your phone?" Dalton asked.

She was surprised by the request. "Sure."

"Have you noticed a light on in the kitchen at the Stevenson house?"

"No, why?"

"I saw a light on last night, but there was no vehicle in the driveway. Figured it might be on a timer of some sort."

"You saw it last night?" He nodded. She scrunched up her forehead, trying to think back. "I honestly don't remember seeing it, but the kitchen overlooks the lake, so I'm not sure I'd notice it from here."

"That's what I thought, too." He took another bite of his French toast. "When Deputy Lewis updated you yesterday, did he say anything about the Stevensons?"

Now she understood why he wanted to use her phone. "No, he didn't. I still don't think Mark or Rich would take a sledgehammer to the gazebo."

He shrugged but didn't say anything more. Jazz knew he didn't agree, but she found it hard to believe that either one of the two sons would care about their small business. As far as she could tell they rarely stayed at the place anyway.

After Dalton called Deputy Lewis, he returned the phone with a glint of satisfaction in his eye. "The deputy agreed to check into the Stevensons to see if they've been around recently. He agrees it's possible they're the ones behind the vandalism."

"It's kids," she insisted. "But whatever. As long as they leave me alone, I don't care if the police find them or not."

"What?" He looked shocked. "Why wouldn't you want to press charges?"

"No reason to give some local kid a criminal record," she pointed out. "It's bad enough that some of the people in town don't like me now, something like that would only add fuel to the fire."

"And if the vandal happens to be an adult?"

"Then I'll press charges," she reluctantly agreed. "Now if you don't mind, I need to clean up the kitchen before we start painting."

"I'll get started," Dalton said. "Meet me when you're ready."

The day passed much like the previous day, with both of them working together to put the second coat of paint on the gazebo. They had a good-natured fight over the radio, which Jazz won. By the time they were finished, the gazebo was a beautiful brilliant white.

"I have an idea," Dalton said, staring at the finished gazebo thoughtfully.

"What's that?"

"This would be a nice spot to hold wedding ceremonies."

Her eyes widened as she envisioned a quaint service being held in the gazebo. "That's an awesome idea. I could hang baskets of flowers along the edge, maybe add tulle for a romantic touch. We could even offer the entire B and B for the wedding party while other guests could stay in the hotel in town."

"Exactly," Dalton agreed. "You could set up various packages online and see what kind of response you get."

She was so thrilled with the plan, she could hardly stand it. Impulsively, she threw her arms around Dalton and hugged him. "This is so great. Why didn't I think of it?"

His arms encircled her, and they shared a poignant embrace before he dropped his arms and stepped back. "I'm sure you would have eventually." He cleared his throat. "Why don't you head inside? I'll finish cleaning up the paint stuff."

"Okay." She entered the house and went directly up to her room. She showered, then went back down to the kitchen to log into The McNallys' B&B website that she'd updated earlier that morning.

But it wasn't there. She frowned, wondering if there was

some weird software glitch. She shut the computer down and then rebooted it.

Still nothing. It was as if the B&B website had never existed.

She stared at the blank page facing her. A chill snaked down her spine. Someone had hacked into her website and wiped it clean. She didn't understand how they'd done something like that, but she knew she'd updated the website that morning and had even tested everything to make sure it was working correctly.

And it had been.

But not anymore. Furious, she picked up her phone and redialed Deputy Lewis.

Apparently, the vandals had found a new way to sabotage her business. Whoever this was clearly wasn't going to give up.

This was too much. She needed the deputy to catch the jerk before he or she could do any more damage either physically to the house or gazebo or electronically.

Wearily, she couldn't help but wonder what the vandal would come up with next.

~

DALTON CAME into the house to find Jazz pacing the length of the kitchen. "What's wrong?"

"Those—mean—awful—argh!" She curled her fingers into fists. "My website has been hacked by the vandals, and they've wiped out *everything*."

He stared in shock. "What? How?"

"I don't know." She spun on her heel and walked away from him. Every inch of her body was in motion. "I still have my domain name, but the website is gone. I'll have to start over from scratch."

"I'm sorry." He truly felt terrible about this latest turn of events. So much for his tent outside keeping the vandalism at bay. They'd only gotten more creative in how to target Jazzlyn. "You should call the Sheriff's Department."

"Deputy Lewis is on his way." She whirled around to face him. "Okay, you were right. This isn't the work of bored kids with nothing to do. This latest attack was a deliberate attempt to sabotage the business."

Being right never felt so awful. "I'm sorry. Do you want me to see if I can fix it?"

"No need. I called my brother Jesse, he's a software guy and will see what he can do for me. But that's not the worst thing about it." She tipped her head back and stared blindly up at the ceiling. "I had reservations built into the website through a special program so both Jemma and I could see them, which means I can't confirm who had already booked rooms for the Memorial Day weekend, not to mention I had several bookings through June."

That wasn't good. "Nothing was backed up?"

Her gaze shot over to clash with his. "I don't even know how to back up a website. It's password protected. I don't have the slightest clue how this scumbag hacked in."

"I see your point," he grudgingly admitted. "Seems like this was done by someone with better than average computer skills. Anyone in particular come to mind?"

"Well, I doubt it's Leon Tate," she muttered. Then her eyes narrowed. "I seem to remember, though, that Rich Stevenson was a computer whiz. He bragged once that he hacked into the FBI computer system. I know it's a stretch, but maybe you were right all along about the Stevenson brothers being a potential suspect."

"That's a great lead." Once again, the temptation to pull her into his arms, holding her close, was nearly overwhelming. He hated knowing that someone was determined to see her business fail. And who knows what lengths these jerks would go to in order to succeed?

A knock at the front door interrupted his thoughts. Jazz rushed over to let Deputy Lewis in. She practically dragged him into the kitchen and pointed to her laptop screen. "It's gone. Completely wiped away. And I just updated it this morning!"

"You're sure you didn't accidently push a wrong button?" Deputy Lewis dropped into a kitchen chair and peered at the screen.

"I'm positive. I'm not an idiot." The edge to her tone betrayed her brittle emotional state. "Even if I didn't save my recent update, there's no possible way to accidently delete the entire website. I don't even know how to do something like that."

"Have you found anything out about the Stevensons?" Dalton asked, trying to deflect Jazz's anger. "Have they been around?"

The deputy shook his head. "I've asked around, no one claims to have seen Mark or Rich recently. I've also left messages for both of them to call me, but so far they haven't."

"What about getting their phone records? Or checking their credit card receipts?" There had to be a way to prove one or both of the Stevensons have been in town. "There has to be something you can do."

Deputy Lewis rose to his feet. "This isn't an episode of *Law and Order*. I need a search warrant for that kind of thing, and other than you seeing someone running into their yard and driving away, there isn't any proof they're involved. No judge is going to grant me access without something more than your opinion."

"What about the fingerprints?" Dalton asked. "Isn't it reasonable to attempt to get a match?"

"Yes, it's reasonable. Which is why I've called and left messages for each of them."

Dalton narrowed his gaze. "Do you really think if you ask them nicely they'll volunteer to come in to be fingerprinted? Yeah, right."

"If they don't cooperate, and if I can prove they've been around, then yes, I could potentially convince a judge to give me a warrant for their fingerprints. But until then? There's not much more I can do."

"Even knowing Rich has the computer skills to do something like this?" Jazz gestured to the blank computer screen.

Deputy Lewis looked pained. "It's not like he's the only one in the entire country with good computer skills. For all we know this could be the work of some overseas hacker. Isn't that where most of the viruses originate?"

Dalton's temper began to simmer. "Come on, first the brick, then the gazebo, and now her website? It's not an overseas hacker, these are all too much of a coincidence. It's clear these various attacks are all targeted specifically at Jazzlyn. Whoever is doing this doesn't want the B and B to be a success."

"I still haven't heard from your former fiancé, Tom Duris," Deputy Lewis said, turning toward Jazz. "You should try calling him. He may return your phone call rather than talking to the police."

Jazz wrinkled her nose as if she detested the idea, but then reluctantly nodded. "Okay, but I'm not sure Tom is knowledgeable enough to wipe out my website either."

"I understand," Deputy Lewis said with a nod. "But at

this point, I'd be thrilled to eliminate even one suspect from the list."

Jazz picked up her phone and stared at it for a minute, her expression clearly portraying her reluctance to make the call. Then she dialed a number she must have had memorized. Tom didn't pick up, so she left a message. "Hi, Tom, it's Jazz. I'd like to talk so please give me a call on my cell." She rattled off the number, then disconnected from the call. She almost looked relieved. "I doubt I'll hear from him."

"Do you have any other way of getting in touch with him?" Deputy Lewis asked. "Email?"

"Yes. I can try that, too." She grimaced. "I guess I could call my former bridesmaid, Megan."

"Why would your friend know where to find Tom?" Dalton asked.

She hesitated as if debating how much to tell them. "Because I believe they're still seeing each other. I caught them kissing after the rehearsal dinner the night before the wedding. It's the reason I called off the ceremony at the last minute."

"Oh, I see." Dalton mentally kicked himself for bringing up such a sensitive subject in front of the deputy.

Grim-faced, Jazz dialed another number, subtly moving away from the two men. Dalton gestured for the deputy to come into the living room to give her privacy.

"I still think the Stevensons are the most likely suspects here," he said in a low tone. "There was a light on in the kitchen last night, but no car in the driveway. Maybe you could have a deputy swing by more often, see if you can catch one of them coming in or out of the house."

"I went over to knock on the door this morning, after you told me about seeing that light. No one answered."

"But if they're trying to hide, they wouldn't answer."

Dalton knew he was acting a bit irrational, but he just had a feeling about the place. "Tell me who else would care about the B and B? The Stevenson house is the closest property and has the most to lose in property value if the McNally twins are successful."

The deputy nodded. "You have a point. I'll post a deputy near the driveway. In the meantime, if you notice anything else out of the ordinary, please let me know."

As far as Dalton could tell, everything about the vandalism against Jazzlyn was out of the ordinary, but he didn't say anything more as Jazz joined them.

"Believe it or not, Megan claims she's not dating Tom any longer and has absolutely no idea where he might be."

"You look surprised," Dalton said.

Jazz nodded. "I am. When I caught them kissing"—she lifted a palm in a helpless gesture—"I assumed they'd been seeing each other for months. Plus, my sister heard they were dating. Megan claims Tom cheated on her, so she dumped him, which really is no surprise."

Dalton couldn't imagine finding your fiancé kissing your best friend. "If he cheated on you, it's no stretch to think he cheated on her."

"You're right." Jazz took a deep breath and then let it out in a whoosh. "Regardless, she doesn't know where Tom is, so all we can do is wait to see if he'll call me back."

"I'll keep an eye on the Stevenson place, too," Deputy Lewis promised. "I'm sorry about your website."

"Me, too." Jazz's expression was gloomy. "I really hope Jesse can fix it."

Her phone rang. She looked at the caller ID, and her shoulders slumped with relief. "My brother," she said as she answered it.

Deputy Lewis edged toward the door, so Dalton followed

him outside. He stood on Jazz's front porch and glanced over at the Stevenson place. From here, he had a fairly clear view of the driveway, although there were a few pine trees separating the two properties, enough that he couldn't quite visualize the front door.

"I'll be in touch," Deputy Lewis said. He walked to the squad car and then slid behind the wheel.

Dalton stared at the Stevenson house, wondering if he should pitch his tent next to the pine tree barrier between the properties so he could keep an eye on the place for himself. It would leave the gazebo vulnerable, though, so he wasn't sure it was worth the risk.

Better to let the sheriff's office keep an eye on the Stevensons. And later that night, he'd go back to sleeping in the tent the way he should have been doing all along.

It was probably the only place on the property that didn't smell like Jazzlyn. Besides, he shouldn't get accustomed to sleeping in a soft bed.

Just as he was turning to go inside, he caught a glimpse of a vehicle driving up the Stevenson driveway. In a heartbeat, he ran over to the edge of the property to get a glimpse of who was behind the wheel.

He figured for sure the driver would be either Mark or Rich, but he was wrong. A beautiful woman slid out from behind the wheel with long curly red hair. She wore a business suit, which he thought was odd.

Before he could approach her, she popped the trunk and walked around to pull something out. It was large and bulky, and it took him a minute to realize it was a For Sale sign.

He pushed between the trees and waved. "Hi! May I ask what you're doing here?"

The woman flashed a thousand-watt smile. "My name is

Melanie Ryerson, and I'm the real estate agent. Are you looking to buy a place?"

"The Stevensons are selling the property?" Dalton knew his assumption about the brothers was dead on. "Are they around? I wouldn't mind talking to them."

"They're not here, but I'm happy to chat with you." Melanie Ryerson was literally beaming with the thought of a quick sale. "I think the price Mr. Stevenson is asking for is reasonable, considering the property sits on the lake."

"Which Mr. Stevenson?" Dalton wanted a name. "Mark or Rich? I know both of them, just curious as to which one hired you."

"Mark, but he did inform me that his brother owns half the property as well." She propped the sign against the side of her sedan and walked toward him with her hand out expectantly. "Nice to meet you, Mr. . . . ."

"O'Brien," he said, taking her hand. "And you may know the owner of the McNally Mansion, Ms. Jazzlyn McNally."

"Yes, I tried to convince her to list the property with me after her grandmother passed away. But she said her family wasn't interested in selling." Melanie brightened. "Do you think they'd like to buy this house, too?"

Dalton doubted that either Jazz or her siblings could afford to buy the place. And that wasn't the point. Knowing the Stevensons had listed the house mere moments after Jazzlyn's website crashed was another coincidence.

One he wasn't about to ignore.

9

Her brother was a genius, at least when it came to computer software. Not only was Jesse able to rebuild her website, but he found the emails imbedded in the previous website that had been sent to her guests confirming their reservations. Since he was working on it, she asked him to add a personal email as well, so that was another task checked off her to-do list. She still needed to reenter the updates she'd done early that morning, but at least the B&B website was back up and running.

Jesse had changed her log-in name and password, too. Hopefully, the additional level of security meant the vandal couldn't break in and create havoc with her website again.

Crisis averted. She let out a deep breath and relaxed. Her stomach rumbled with hunger. Dalton had spackled the drywall in the blue room while she'd been on the phone with her brother, and when he'd finished that, he'd come downstairs and insisted on cooking dinner.

He'd chosen something simple, hamburgers and a salad, but she didn't mind. Any food she didn't have to cook was a bonus in her book. Besides, after everything that had happened, she was extremely grateful to have Dalton around.

If she'd been here alone with all this going on—she suppressed a shiver, unsure how she would have handled the series of disasters without support.

This latest attack on her business was truly upsetting. Especially since she had no idea what the vandal would do next. Physical damage was one thing, but cyber damage was something else. No ordinary person could be skillful at both of them.

Could they?

"Here you go," Dalton said, bringing over a plate full of juicy hamburgers.

"Thanks, Dalton," she murmured with a weary smile. "They look delicious."

"Normally I'm the king of grilling out, but I didn't see one outside." He dropped into the chair across from her at the table.

She glanced up. "I didn't realize the campsites have grills for you to use."

He froze for a nanosecond, then slowly nodded. "Some of them do." Averting his gaze, he reached for a burger and took a bite.

She had the impression that his claim of being king of the grilling had been a reference to a previous life, not the drifter one he was living now. Swallowing her curiosity about his past wasn't easy. "The only meal we're offering on a regular basis is breakfast, so there isn't a desperate need for a grill. But maybe once we're settled in we can add that to our wish list."

Dalton nodded, his expression guarded. "Speaking of campsites, I plan on sleeping in the tent tonight. Better to be outside in case there's another attempt on the gazebo. I still believe the Stevenson brothers are the ones behind all this."

Two people, one attacking her property, the other waging a cyberattack. She couldn't disagree with his assumption that the Stevenson brothers were the prime suspects.

Would they keep coming after her? Even now? The thought of her beautifully and freshly painted gazebo being broken to smithereens made her feel sick to her stomach. Yet at the same time, she didn't like the idea of Dalton placing himself in danger.

"It's certainly starting to look as if Mark and Rich are the masterminds behind this," she agreed, taking another bite of her hamburger. Hmm, delicious. "Our families were never close, the way you would think they should be, even with the age differences. Rich and Mark never wanted anything to do with us kids and went out of their way to make sure we weren't welcome at their get-togethers. Add to that how they've recently put their house on the market . . ." She shrugged.

"They're probably hoping they can sell it off before your business is up and running," Dalton said. "I've asked Deputy Lewis to make sure he has a deputy stationed nearby to watch the place tonight."

She couldn't hide her relief. "That's great news. And since there will be a cop nearby, there's absolutely no reason for you to sleep in the tent."

Once again, he averted his gaze as if his burger was something to be studied. "I'd rather sleep outside; it's no problem."

"Trying to avoid me, huh?" She'd meant to sound teasing, but that's not how the words came out of her mouth. They hung in the air, shimmering with hurt.

Dalton lifted his eyes to meet hers, his gaze serious. "Nothing has changed, Jazz. I'm only staying long enough to get the renovations done, then I'll be on my way."

"Yes, you've mentioned that. A few times now." She tried to hide her annoyance. "Makes me wonder, exactly which one of us are you trying to convince?"

He hesitated and shrugged. "Both of us. I never thought I'd like working with a partner, but I like working with you. Maybe too much."

Her heart skipped a beat. "I like working with you, too. And I'm glad you're here, Dalton. Not just for the heavy physical work, but because I really enjoy your company. I think we make a great team."

He flinched as if she'd slapped him. "That's exactly the problem. You're making a life for yourself here. But for me, this is nothing more than a pleasant interlude."

"Your choice, Dalton." She was tired of pussy-footing around the subject of his past. "You could choose to stay and build a life for yourself, too. If not here, then somewhere else. Haven't you figured out by now that you can't run away from your problems? They'll follow you regardless of how fast and far you choose to run."

His cheeks flushed, and his eyes turned dark with repressed anger. "You don't know *anything* about my problems."

"Only because you haven't shared them with me." Her tone was laced with frustration. "You know the truth about what I've been going through. I've told you I called off my wedding the night before the ceremony because I caught my ex-fiancé cheating with my bridesmaid after the rehearsal dinner. You also know my sister is having problems with her ex-husband."

He didn't say anything in response.

"I'm right here, Dalton," she said encouragingly. "I'm ready and willing to listen if you decide you'd like to talk."

He was silent for another full minute. She figured he'd finish his meal and disappear when he softly said, "Talking about it won't bring them back."

Them? As in more than one person? Her stomach clenched with dread. "Who?"

Another infinitely long pause. "My wife and six-month-old son."

"Oh, Dalton." She reached across the table and placed her hand over his. Her heart ached for what he'd been through. "I'm so sorry for your loss."

He stared down at her hand covering his for a moment, then shook off her touch, leaning back in his seat as if to keep his distance. "I'm sorry, too. Because the worst part is, I'm the one who caused their deaths."

"I don't believe that," she said, instinctively denying his claim.

"You should," he said in a harsh tone. He abruptly stood, leaving his half-eaten second burger on his plate. "Because it's true. My wife and my son died because of me."

He disappeared into the master bedroom for less than a minute before heading outside. He closed the French doors behind him, and she watched as he crawled inside the small red tent.

Jazz drew in a deep breath and let it out slowly. He'd finally told her the truth, but she didn't feel better knowing he'd lost his wife and young son. And she suspected he didn't feel any better either.

In fact, she sensed she'd only made things worse.

He seemed so convinced that he was at fault. The Dalton she'd come to know over these past several days couldn't have done anything harmful to anyone. Quite the opposite. Dalton had proved himself to be considerate and protective.

But what did she really know about the man he'd been before he'd become a drifter?

Absolutely nothing.

Sleeping on the cold hard ground after a couple of days in a nice warm bed was pure torture. How in the world had he gotten so soft, so fast?

Dalton had no idea but sternly told himself to get over it. He didn't deserve warmth and comfort. Not anymore.

And what possessed him to tell Jazz about how he'd lost his wife and son? He hadn't told anyone along his drifter journey about his past life, keeping the secret closely guarded deep in his heart.

He still couldn't believe he'd babbled to Jazz. Not all the gory details about the extent of his failure, but enough. He took some comfort in the fact that she would now under-stand why he couldn't stay to make a life for himself here in McNally Bay the way she'd suggested.

No matter how tempting it was to try to do just that.

Wait a minute, what was he thinking? Sure, this was a nice place and he enjoyed being on the water. But staying near Jazzlyn would be dangerous on an emotional level.

He was having a difficult enough time keeping his hands off her as it was.

Kissing was off-limits, remember?

He rolled over in his sleeping bag, wincing as his hip landed on a rock. He shifted to one side and then tried to fall asleep.

His eyes shot open, and he stared at the nylon side of his tent. Sleep was obviously not happening.

Dalton crawled out of the tent, the cold air wrapping around him like an icy blanket. Maybe if he walked the property for a while he'd wear himself out. Physical exertion was a strategy that had worked well for him in the past.

The sound of the water was soothing. He rounded the gazebo and noticed the small kitchen light was glowing again. It had to be on a timer, but he headed toward the Stevenson place anyway.

Aside from the light, there was no sign of anyone living there. He looked up at the Stevenson house and imagined building a screened in porch spanning the entire length of the house, overlooking the lake. Up close he could see that the wooden siding was chipped and peeling. When was the last time the brothers had painted the place?

Now that he thought about it, it was surprising that the home hadn't been changed at all in what appeared to be at least thirty years, maybe more. Why hadn't the Stevenson brothers put any money into updating it?

Was the inside as old-fashioned looking as the outside? If so, the price of the home wouldn't be nearly as high as he originally assumed.

Although what did it matter? It wasn't as if he was looking to buy the place. When he'd walked away from his old life, he'd left whatever money he'd had socked away behind. And he hadn't touched a dime of it.

No reason to start thinking about ways to spend it now.

Shaking off the idea of buying and rebuilding, he rounded the corner toward the front of the house. No cars were parked in the driveway, which wasn't a surprise. He stood for a moment, wondering how far down the road the deputy had parked.

Too far away to see him, obviously. Which meant he'd made a good decision to sleep in the tent.

He turned and made his way back to Jazz's house, checking that her driveway and garage were undisturbed. It occurred to him that the next target could very well be the garage. The building wasn't attached to the house and could be accessed by anyone walking down the driveway.

Feeling a bit grim, he realized that sleeping in the tent couldn't prevent all potential vandalism. Keeping the gazebo safe, sure, but the rest of the house was fair game. Including the garage that Jazz hoped to use as a foundation for an upper apartment.

The structure was huge, and he took a moment to pace it off to estimate the square footage of the base of the building. It was larger than he'd originally thought at sixty feet long and forty feet wide. Then he stood up against the building and tried to figure out how tall it was. The typical garage was eight feet high, maybe nine at the most. Jazz's garage was much higher. He wondered if this particular outbuilding was made taller in hopes of storing large stuff like a recreational vehicle or a large boat. His internal architect eye guesstimated that it was easily fourteen feet tall.

If Jazz didn't raise the roof, the apartment would be smaller in height, walls that were only six feet high instead of the normal eight feet. The cost of raising the roof may be prohibitive of getting the project done, especially since she'd hoped to do that sooner versus later.

Considering the only occupants of the apartment were likely to be Jazz's twin and her young son, maybe they could make do with the shorter walls.

He could design it both ways so that Jazz would understand the difference.

Whoa, wait a minute. He didn't design buildings any

longer. He was a simple construction worker. Besides, even if he wanted to design something, he didn't have a drafting table or any of his tools.

Still, he could put a few basic designs together. A starting point if not enough to build from. They could be his parting gift to Jazz. He stared at the garage again for several long moments until the chilly wind made him shiver.

Enough. He needed to get some sleep. Completing the circle around Jazz's property brought him back to the tent where he'd started. He forced himself to crawl back inside, even though every fiber of his being begged him to go inside where it was warm and comfy.

Dalton tossed and turned throughout the rest of the night. He dozed on and off, the chill seeping through his sleeping bag bringing him awake more often than not, as if his body couldn't seem to stand the cold for another second.

At dawn, he gave up any attempt to stay strong and pathetically crawled into the house. He made his way to the kitchen, basking in the warmth as he brewed a pot of coffee.

He didn't want to disturb Jazz, so he carried his mug of coffee into the bathroom she'd designated for him to use and soaked in a hot shower. When he finished, he decided to launder one set of his clothes, along with the towels.

After a brief internal debate, he decided against starting breakfast, unsure what time Jazz had gone to bed. He searched through the small desk Jazz had set up in the living room until he found a pad of drawing paper and pencils.

At the kitchen table, he picked up the pencil and stared at the blank sheet of paper, envisioning the garage. The pencil felt like a natural extension of his fingers, which was a bit unnerving considering how long it had been since he'd done any drawing.

Guess it was just like riding a bike.

He quickly drew the dimensions of the garage as the starting floor plan. Then he sketched a kitchen, living area, and two bedrooms separated by a bathroom.

An hour later, he sat back, satisfied with his design. He'd added all the basic essentials, identifying exactly where the appliances would go, making sure there would be adequate closet space and enough room for a full bathroom between the two bedrooms.

He could easily imagine Jazz's twin sister and her son living up there.

Not that he'd be around to see it for himself. He set the design aside, figuring the basic floor plan would work regardless of the ceiling height.

Hearing muffled thuds from upstairs spurred him into action. He searched in the fridge for eggs and bacon and set about making breakfast. When they'd finished eating he'd head upstairs to check the spackle he'd added yesterday, before tackling the tile in the yellow room. The old stuff had to be removed before he could estimate how much work would be needed to repair the walls behind it.

They'd lost some time yesterday after the computer issue, but he was determined to make up for it today.

"Good morning," Jazz said as she entered the kitchen. "I thought I was dreaming when I woke up to the scent of coffee."

He glanced over at her, his heart thudding in his chest at how beautiful she looked. Granted, he'd never seen her wearing anything but jeans and sweatshirt, but it didn't matter. It was the light in her eyes and the brightness of her smile that drew him in.

Like a siren's song, he found her incredibly hard to resist.

"Bacon and eggs, my favorite." Jazz brushed against him as she moved toward the coffee pot. "But you didn't have to cook breakfast. It was my turn considering you made dinner last night."

He shrugged and forced himself to concentrate on the food he was making. "Doesn't matter, I'm not keeping count. Besides, I was up early this morning."

She eyed him curiously over the rim of her mug. "Gee, did that have anything to do with you insisting on sleeping out in the freezing cold?"

He chuckled wryly. "Probably. Have a seat, the bacon will be ready in a few minutes. The eggs won't take long."

Jazz nodded and dropped into a chair. "What is this?" she asked, pulling his drawing toward her.

He could feel the tips of his ears burning with embarrassment. "It's, um, just a sketch of what the garage apartment might look like."

"A sketch?" Her tone was incredulous. "It's more than that, it looks like an actual floor plan."

He stirred the scrambled eggs, wishing her admiration didn't mean so much to him. "It's rough because I don't have my tools."

"Tools?" Her confusion was obvious, and he mentally smacked himself upside the head for saying anything.

"The eggs are just about ready," he said in a weak attempt to change the subject. "How many slices of bacon would you like?"

"Three. I'm starving." Jazz waited until he'd filled two plates with food and carried them over to place one in front of her. "What kind of tools?"

He sighed, sensing she wasn't going to let it go. "Drafting tools."

"Drafting?" She wrinkled her brow. "I don't know anything about it."

"They're small instruments used by architects to design

buildings. They have measurements along the sides that convert inches to feet so drawings can be made to scale."

"You're an architect!" Jazz exclaimed. "I should have figured that out before now. No wonder you know so much about doing construction."

"I was an architect," he corrected. "I don't design stuff anymore. Now, I'm a handyman."

She frowned. "Once an architect, always an architect."

"No." The denial came out stronger than he intended. "Enough poking into my past, Jazz."

She looked taken aback, but then reluctantly nodded. "Okay, sorry."

"Apology accepted." He dug into his meal, intending to eat as quickly as possible so he could start ripping out tile.

But he couldn't help but notice the way Jazz continued to gaze at his sketch with blatant admiration. And for the first time in over a year, he found himself missing the work and career he'd walked away from.

———

10

Architect. Dalton O'Brien was an architect. She stared in awe at the floor plan he'd created for her. The garage apartment design that Dalton had drawn was so precise, Jazz couldn't believe he'd done it freehand.

Clearly, he didn't want to talk about his career any more than he'd wanted to talk about how he'd lost his wife and young son.

She wished she understood why the two subjects caused him so much pain. Well, she understood how losing a wife and son would be incredibly painful, but how did being an architect factor in? The two issues didn't seem connected, at least from what she could tell.

They finished their breakfast in silence, each apparently lost in their thoughts. Jazz took small comfort in the way Dalton had opened up, even a little bit, about his past. The picture in her head was becoming clearer with every bread-crumb that he dropped.

He'd grilled out for his family, probably on the week-ends. He'd loved his wife and son and seemingly enjoyed a great career as an architect.

What sorts of buildings had he designed? Did architects specialize in one thing or another? They must, because designing a skyscraper office building had to be very different from laying out a hospital or school.

She wanted to ask, but Dalton had point-blank told her not to poke her nose into his past, so she held back.

Dalton finished his breakfast before she did. He rose to his feet and took his dirty dishes to the sink. "I'd like to start tearing out the old tile this morning, if that's okay with you."

"Oh, sure. Although I can do that if there's drywall stuff that has yet to be done."

"The spackle is dry, and the walls are ready for primer," he acknowledged. "I figured that might be an easier job for you to tackle. Unless you're a whiz at caulking tile?"

She almost choked on her coffee. "Um, no. I'm not a whiz at caulking tile. I'd like to learn how to do it, though."

He shrugged. "It's actually not that hard, but first we have to get the old stuff down. Peeling away the ceramic is easy, but getting rid of the old mud behind it will take quite a bit of elbow grease."

"That and sheer determination and thinking about my grandpa as I work is how I made it this far," Jazz said. She popped the last piece of bacon in her mouth, then stood. "Tell you what, you start on the tile in the blue room, and I'll work on the bathroom in the yellow room." She flashed him a cheeky grin. "We'll race to see who gets finished faster."

"No contest," he scoffed. "I'll have you beaten by hours."

"You think so, huh?" She liked the lighter teasing side of Dalton. "Don't be too sure. I tend to imagine my ex-fiancé's face when I do demolition work."

He burst out laughing at that. "Duly noted. Let's wash

the dishes together first, before we tackle our respective bathrooms. We have to be sure we start at the same time so there's no cheating."

She huffed out a breath. "I never cheat."

His eyes gleamed. "Me either. But I like to win."

Washing the breakfast dishes didn't take long, and they both walked up to the second-floor bedrooms together. Jazz armed herself with a putty knife and disappeared into the yellow room. The moment she began chipping away at the old tile she could hear the same sound coming from the blue room.

The race was on.

Jazz hadn't considered herself to be competitive by nature, but she attacked the tile with a frenzy, determined to give Dalton a run for his money.

Not that they had any money on the table, this little race to the finish wasn't about that.

Actually, now that she thought about it, she wasn't sure what the point was.

But that didn't stop her from putting every ounce of effort into the task. Within twenty minutes she found a good rhythm. Until she ran into a tiny problem. The high tiles were difficult to reach, and she wasted several precious minutes fetching a ladder so she could get at them.

Two hours later the last tile fell away, and she rushed out of the yellow room to find Dalton.

"I'm finished," she announced as she poked her head into the blue room bathroom.

Dalton was literally on the last tile, and it hit the floor of the tub with a resounding crack. He stared at her in surprise. "I can't believe you beat me!"

"Well, I did." She did a little dance, not the least bit embarrassed to gloat. "Loser buys lunch."

"We didn't bet on lunch," he protested with a smile. "But that's okay, I don't mind buying."

She leaned against the doorjamb, suddenly feeling exhausted, her arm muscles aching from the exertion. "I'm surprised there isn't any black mold behind the tile in here," she observed. "The walls in the yellow bathroom look good, too."

"Added bonus," Dalton agreed. "We can sand down the wall to get rid of the old grout, then reseal it before putting up new tile. Should look great when it's all finished."

She nodded, easily picturing it in her mind's eye. "I already have a belt sander, so that's good. But I would like to head into town to buy new tile and grout. Plus, I'd like some new fixtures, ones that look old-fashioned enough to fit in with the antique feel of the house."

"Understood." Dalton stretched, and she found herself mesmerized by the way the T-shirt clung to his chest. What was it about Dalton's muscles that she found so attractive? She really needed to get a grip. "Grab the belt sander for me, will you? We may need additional supplies for it."

"Sure." She tore her gaze away from his chest and turned to find the sander he'd left in the main bedroom. She stood for a moment, willing her heartbeat to return to normal.

This ridiculous adolescent-like crush she had on Dalton had to stop. Hadn't she been hurt enough by Tom's betrayal?

Emotions in check, Jazz brought over the sander to Dalton. He plugged it in and used it on one portion of the wall. It worked great, but she could tell that the old grout would wear through the belts far more quickly than it had the drywall seams. They needed more to get through two bathrooms.

"I'll add belts to the list," she said. "Tile, grout, sandpaper, and fixtures. The lights are decent, so I'm not swapping those out yet." She swept a gaze over the partially demolished bathroom. "Anything else?"

"Do you have paint for the blue room? And enough for the respective bathrooms?"

She shook her head. "No, I'll add that. I want to do one wall navy blue, the rest white in both the bathroom and the bedroom. The furnishings will be mostly white with navy-blue accents."

"Nice," Dalton said with approval.

She smiled. "Thanks. The green room was my favorite growing up, but by the time I'm done in here, I might like the blue room better. Let's hit the hardware store so I can put another big dent in my renovation budget."

There had to be something wrong with her, because the hardware/home-improvement store was fast becoming her favorite place to hang out. She sent Dalton off to find the sandpaper belts while she mulled over paint chips. When she'd found the navy blue, white, and soft yellow paint she needed to finish up the two rooms, she wheeled the cart over to the bathroom tile.

There were way too many choices, but she found the perfect design for the blue room right away. The next choice took longer, and Dalton had joined her by the time she picked out the tile she liked for the yellow room.

"White grout is probably best," he said. "Harder to keep clean, but we'll seal it well enough that it should hold up without a problem."

"White grout it is." She added that to her cart. "Next up, plumbing fixtures."

Another area full of difficult choices, but she managed to find what she wanted. At the checkout counter, she tried not to wince at the total.

"Where would you like to go for lunch?" Dalton asked once they were in the truck. "Back to Daisy's Diner?"

"Sure." She drove down Main Street and turned into the diner. Seeing the ATM machine made her realize how much she still owed Dalton for the work he'd put in over the past few days. "I'll meet you inside, okay?"

He nodded and slid out from the passenger seat. She darted across the street toward the ATM, returning moments later. Dalton waited outside the diner but waved her away when she tried to pay him. "That's too much. The way you're feeding me, I can't accept what we originally agreed upon."

"That's ridiculous. Having you at the house has been a tremendous help. I wouldn't be even close to being finished without you."

His face was set in a stubborn line. "Cut the amount in half and we'll call it a day."

He was letting her off easy, but she sensed he wasn't about to change his mind, so she did as he asked. He tucked the bills into the pocket of his jeans and then opened the door.

The diner wasn't as full as it had been the previous day, but she still stopped short when she recognized Leon Tate seated at one of the booths. There was a familiar woman seated across from him, and it took a moment for Jazz to place her.

"I don't believe it," she muttered.

Dalton misinterpreted her reaction. "Don't worry, we'll stay far away from that jerk."

"From both of them." At Dalton's confused expression she tipped her chin toward the couple. "See that woman across from him? I'm not sure what her relationship is to him, she looks too young to be his wife. Anyway, she

rammed her cart into me at the grocery store, hard enough
to knock me off my feet."

"What? Unbelievable," Dalton said in a harsh tone.
"That's assault."

"Yeah, well, she denied it anyway." He moved toward
Leon Tate's table, but she grabbed his arm in a tight grip.
"Let it go, Dalton. They're not worth it."

He finally agreed and led the way to an empty booth.
She took a seat across from him, curious about who the
younger woman was. A daughter? A niece? Surely not
his wife.

If Leon Tate was competitive with her father, the way
Mrs. Cromwell claimed, that only explained his crabby attitude. She still couldn't figure out how the old man's anger
would transfer to the younger woman.

Somehow, she sensed there was more to the animosity
Leon Tate felt toward her family than simple competi-
tiveness.

DALTON WANTED nothing more than to confront the old
man but held back the way Jazz had asked him to. After
all, she would be here in McNally Bay long after he
was gone.

A fact that continued to gnaw at him, no matter how
much he reminded himself how much he liked his life just
the way it was.

The problem was that he didn't want to leave Jazz. And
that scared him to death.

He was distracted from his troublesome thoughts by
Leon Tate walking slowly past their booth, leaning heavily
on his cane. Dalton braced himself for the worst, deter-

mined to protect Jazz if the jerk said anything derogatory or spiteful.

This time, he wouldn't hesitate the give the old geezer a piece of his mind.

But he needn't have worried. Jazz looked the old man directly in the eye and smiled brightly. "Good afternoon, Mr. Tate. Wonderful weather we're having, isn't it? Hope you both have a nice day."

Leon and the woman behind him looked surprised, knocked completely off balance at the cheerfulness of Jazz's tone. Dalton choked back a laugh as the Tates glanced at each other, then moved past without saying anything.

"There you go. My dad always taught us to kill them with kindness," Jazz said with satisfaction. Then she pointed at him. "Although you almost blew it by laughing in their face."

"I'm sorry, but I wasn't expecting you to greet them like that." He chuckled. "Have to say, it was pretty funny to watch them struggle not to respond in kind."

She beamed. "Right? I loved it. But hey, there's always next time."

Only next time, he might not be there to see it. Maybe he could stick around for a while longer. See if anyone else in town needed some handyman work done.

Ashley, the same server they had last time they were in, came over. As before, she looked harried. "Lemonade and iced tea?"

"Good memory," Dalton said. "Works for me. Jazz?"

"Make it two lemonades. I wouldn't want to be too predictable."

"Ashley, who was that woman with Mr. Tate?" Dalton asked. "His daughter?"

"Yes, her name is Mary Tate, and she's been staying with

Leon ever since his wife passed away from cancer." Ashley's smile was distracted. "Let me get those drinks for you, then I'll take your lunch order."

"I'm not surprised they're related," Jazz said thoughtfully. "Although that still doesn't explain why on earth she felt the need to run into me with a shopping cart."

"No idea." Dalton didn't like knowing that the Tates had struck out against Jazz. He firmly believed the Stevenson brothers were the masterminds behind the vandalism, but there was obviously something else going on in this small town.

He wished he knew what it was.

A glance at the white board confirmed the special of the day was shepherd's pie. Sounded good to him. When Ashley returned with their drinks, he asked for the special and so did Jazz.

His stomach rumbled loudly, making Jazz grin.

"Glad your appetite has returned."

He shouldn't have been surprised by her astute observation. "I'm sure the hard work we've been doing has helped."

"Really?" She lifted a bow, regarding him curiously. "Are you saying you didn't work hard for Mrs. Cromwell?"

He frowned. "Of course, I did."

She leaned forward, propping her elbows on the table. "Dalton, when I met you, your clothes hung off your frame as if you hadn't eaten a decent meal in months. Since you've started working with me, you've been chowing down food like crazy. And it's a good thing. I'm glad you've put on a couple of pounds over the past few days. It suits you."

Her admiration was difficult to ignore. He curled his fingers into fists, aching to haul her across the table and into his arms.

There was something about Jazz that called to him in a way he hadn't experienced since meeting Debbie.

"Um, thanks. I think." He could feel the tips of his ears burning, so he changed the subject. "After lunch, I'll start sanding the bathroom in the yellow room, if you want to begin painting in the blue room. It's best if the painting in the main bedroom is finished before dust starts to fly."

"Sounds like a plan," Jazz agreed. "I'm an expert at painting by now."

In his humble opinion, she was an expert in a lot of things, especially home renovation. "You're an incredible woman, Jazz."

This time it was her turn to blush, and the pinkness of her cheeks made her green eyes sparkle. He reached across the table to cover her hand in his, but before he could say anything, Ashley came out of the kitchen carrying a tray.

"Two shepherd's pies," she announced. "Careful, the cast iron pot is really hot."

He reluctantly released Jazz's hand and sat back against the seat so Ashley had room to set down their meals. The shepherd's pie came with a mini-loaf of brown bread.

"Very Irish," he said in admiration.

Ashley's smile was wan. "Yeah, I wouldn't know. But it definitely tastes good."

"Have you been to Ireland?" Jazz asked as she poked her fork through the crispy potato covering the pie.

"No, but my grandmother immigrated from Ireland, and she was a great cook."

"Kind of funny that we're both Irish," Jazz said. "And immigrants at that."

"True." He took a small bite. "Hmm. This is tasty, but can't touch my Nana's."

"Is your grandmother still around?"

"No. She passed away five years ago now. But she was an incredible cook. And an amazing woman." He missed his Nana and once again thought about the fact that he hadn't been in touch with his parents since Debbie's and Davy's funerals.

"I've thought about tracing my Irish roots," Jazz went on. "Family history is so incredibly interesting, isn't it? Maybe I could trace your grandmother's heritage, too."

"Maybe." He knew his tone lacked enthusiasm.

They finished their meal, and he paid Ashley, leaving a nice tip because he had a sense the young woman needed a bit of extra cash.

Driving back to the McNally Mansion didn't take long. "I'll carry in the boxes of tile, you grab the paint."

"I'm strong enough to carry tile," Jazz protested.

"If you drop them, they'll shatter."

She rolled her eyes and reached for the paint. "Fine, but make sure you don't drop them either."

"I won't." He made three trips to the truck until he had all the tile up in the respective bathrooms. As he returned to the main level, he could hear Jazz talking on the phone.

"Really? That's great, Jemma. I'm thrilled you'll be here in just two more weeks."

Two weeks? Dalton hesitated, a sharp pain stabbing deep into his chest, right in the spot where his heart once sat.

Sounds as if Jazz's twin will be coming out to join her in two weeks. Which is great for Jazz because now she can open rooms earlier than originally planned.

And he'd need to move his things out of the master suite.

Jazz came rushing out of the kitchen. "Dalton! Jemma is quitting her teaching job early! She'll be here in two weeks."

"I heard," he said, forcing a smile. "That's great news."

"It's all because of you." Jazz threw her arms around his neck and hugged him tight. "Thank you, Dalton. Thank you so much!"

He clutched her close, loving the way the softness of her body molded to his. She felt perfect in his arms, as if she belonged there.

He wanted her. More than he thought possible. He tipped her chin up and slowly, deliberately, captured her mouth with his.

11

D alton's kiss was incredible, a rock amidst a stormy sea. Jazz clung to him, hoping and praying he'd never let her go.

But of course, he did. Still, he didn't push her away as he'd done previously. Keeping his arms wrapped around her, he lifted his head and gazed intently at her face, almost as if he were memorizing what she looked like.

"Wow," she murmured. "That was amazing."

"Yeah, it was." He pressed his lips against her temple. "I wish . . ." His voice trailed off, and she would have given up her portion of the B&B to hear what he'd been about to say.

He didn't finish his thought.

She swallowed against a lump of frustration. Yes, he was allowed to grieve over losing his wife and son. Yes, he had the right to live his life as a drifter if that's what he really wanted.

But she didn't for one minute believe that to be the case.

Dalton hadn't *chosen* to live his life as a drifter moving from one spot to another. He was doing it out of guilt. For whatever he'd supposedly done to cause their deaths.

The worst scenario she could think of was driving while intoxicated and causing a crash that had claimed their lives. It seemed out of character for the man she'd come to know, but maybe things had been different a year ago.

Regardless, he'd suffered more than enough.

"Do you think your wife would want you to live alone for the rest of your life?"

He stiffened against her but didn't pull away as she half expected him too. "I'm not sure, but it's what I deserve."

"And would she agree with you about that?" she pressed. "Would your wife think you deserve to live a lonely existence drifting from one place to another living in a tent?"

"Probably." He grimaced and loosened his grip. She didn't move away from him, though. She grasped his shoulders, wishing she could shake some sense into him.

"I don't believe you. A woman you loved couldn't possibly be that vindictive."

He looked startled by her comment. "Debbie wasn't at all vindictive. She was wonderful. I didn't deserve her."

"Dalton." She let out a heavy sigh. "You must realize no one is perfect. We all make mistakes. Maybe you screwed up, but I'm willing to bet there were mistakes Debbie made, too. The whole concept of marriage is give and take. Compromise. Learn to focus on the good and downplay the bad."

He lifted a brow. "Says the woman who walked away from her groom the night before the wedding."

"True. But that only proves my point. I made mistakes and so did Tom. In our case, some of them were bigger than others, like Tom's mistake in kissing my bridesmaid."

"That's not your fault," Dalton swiftly interjected. The way he jumped to her defense was sweet.

"It was partially my fault because I mistook affection for

love. I never should have agreed to marry him in the first place." She cupped his cheek with her hand. "I finally figured out that Tom didn't really love me and I didn't love him. If you want to know the truth, Tom's kisses never made me feel half as special as yours do."

"Don't say that," he protested. "You're killing me, Jazz," he added in a low husky voice.

"Ditto," she countered. Moving up on her tippy toes, she pressed a soft, sweet kiss against his lips. "Now, it's time to get to work."

He stared at her for another moment, before nodding and turning away. Wondering what he was thinking would only drive her crazy, so Jazz tried to push her insatiable curiosity out of her mind.

Setting up for painting took a while, but once she had everything draped and the woodwork protected with tape, she went to work.

She used the white paint first, covering the light blue that had been on the walls previously. Her back ached from leaning backward on the ladder to do the ceiling, but her efforts were well worth it.

The sound of Dalton using the electric sander in the yellow room, a loud humming noise behind her eighties tunes, brought an odd comfort. She was becoming so used to having him around; he'd leave a gaping hole in her life when he decided to leave.

Was there any possible way to convince him to stay? As soon as the thought teased her mind, she shook her head. Nope. Dalton had to be the one to make a choice. A decision. Battling through his guilt and memories of the past long enough to find a way to forgive himself.

Only then would he be able to move on.

At least Jemma would be coming sooner than originally planned. Her twin and nephew would help fill the gap created by Dalton's leaving. She'd have to fill Jemma in on the weird dynamics between the McNallys and the Tates. Maybe after they got to know more of the locals on a first-name basis, she'd be able to understand the source of Leon Tate's animosity.

The bedrooms weren't large, so she managed to finish up the first coat close to dinnertime. She stood in the center of the room, swinging her hips to "We Got the Beat" by the Go-Go's, and surveyed her work. Not bad. Since she'd chosen the navy-blue wall to be the one behind the headboard of the four-poster bed, she began shifting the furniture around so she could start on that one in the morning.

The power sanding had stopped an hour earlier, so when she finished in the blue room, she walked over to check on Dalton's progress.

The bathroom walls were smooth and ready for new tile. Dalton had cleaned up all the dust and had replaced the fixtures on the sink. The ones for the shower were set off on the side, ready to go once the tile work was completed.

Dalton wasn't anywhere around, so she headed downstairs to look for him. He wasn't in the main living area, nor was he in the kitchen.

Dark clouds gathering outside drew her attention. She moved closer to gauge the potential storm when she caught a glimpse of Dalton heading over to the Stevensons'. Had one of the brothers finally showed up?

She hurried outside to catch up with Dalton but slowed her pace when she saw a tall, beautiful redhead greeting him with a warm handshake. The stab of jealousy was ridiculous but didn't stop her from smoothing a hand over her hair, hoping there weren't too many white paint flecks clinging to the dark strands.

The redhead saw her and waved her over. "Oh, you must be Jazzlyn McNally! We've talked on the phone, remember?"

"We have?" Jazz asked wryly, as she crossed the lawn to meet them. News to her.

"Yes, after your grandmother passed away."

"Oh yes. That was a difficult time," Jazz murmured.

The woman's smile faltered. "Of course. I'm sorry for your loss."

"Jazz, this is Melanie Ryerson," Dalton introduced the redhead. "She's the real estate agent handling the Stevenson property."

"Nice to meet you." Jazz glanced at the house, noticing how run-down it appeared up close. "Are either Mark or Rich here?"

"No, I'm afraid not. But I thought you both would like to take a quick tour, you know, just in case you know of anyone who might be interested in buying a lakefront property."

"My budget is tied up in the B and B," Jazz said in case the realtor assumed she was rolling in dough. "But I'm nosey enough to want to look around."

"Me, too," Dalton said. "Let's take a look before the storm blows in. Have you shown it to many potential buyers?"

"Just one couple so far." The wattage on Melanie's smile dimmed. "There is a bit of work that's needed inside, and they weren't interested in taking on a fixer-upper."

"Renovations are Jazz's specialty," Dalton said, flashing Jazz a grin. "Aren't they?"

"I'm up to my eyeballs in my current project, remember?" She followed Melanie up onto the porch and into the house. A dank, musty smell made her wrinkle her nose. "This place could use a good airing out."

"True, but look at all the potential here." Melanie's attitude was undaunted as she gestured to the living room.

"All I see is water damage on the ceiling," Jazz said. "I'm assuming there must be a bathroom upstairs?"

"Yes, two of them actually. One in the master bedroom and one placed between two smaller bedrooms." Melanie beamed. "You know, it's not easy to find a house this size with three bathrooms, not to mention two-and-a-half baths."

Jazz exchanged a look with Dalton. Melanie Ryerson was a saleswoman through and through. No doubt she'd attempt to sell bottled sand to people living in the desert.

"The kitchen is right here." Melanie led the way into a smallish kitchen area with a large dining room attached. "Look at the view of the lake!"

Again, in her point of view, it was a waste of space to have the dining room overlooking the lakefront. A room with a view should be the living room, not a formal dining room used only on rare occasions.

"Who designed this place anyway?" Jazz whispered to Dalton.

He chuckled and shook his head. "Not a skilled architect, that's for sure."

"The kitchen cabinets could be repainted," Melanie continued. "New counters and appliances would also work wonders in here."

"Kitchen remodels are pricey," Jazz commented. "I can see why a young couple would be intimidated by a project this size."

Melanie's smile grew brittle. "Considering the location, this place is a hidden gem." She opened the door to the combined laundry area and main floor powder room that was generally okay. Then she led the way upstairs to the second floor.

The master bedroom looked decent enough; the bathroom was outdated, but otherwise functional. It was the second full bathroom between the two guest rooms that was a complete disaster. Clearly it had flooded more than once, the linoleum on the floor was bubbled and curled. In the spots where she could see the subfloor, she caught a glimpse of what appeared to be black mold.

"This room would need to be completely gutted, down to the studs," Dalton said as if reading her mind. "The floor could be rotten, so you should watch your step in here. Bring anyone in weighing over two hundred and fifty pounds and you'll likely find him on the floor in the living room below."

Melanie's temper flared. "Are you purposefully trying to upset me? I thought you would appreciate knowing the potential here, but apparently all you care about is pointing out its flaws."

"We're only being realistic," Jazz said in a soothing voice. "Trust me, a home inspector will find all of this and more."

"Hrmph." Melanie spun on her heel and walked down to the main level. When she and Dalton joined her, she led the way outside, clearly anxious to get rid of her visitors. She flashed a fake smile. "If you know of anyone interested in buying, please give me a call."

"Sure," Jazz agreed. "Thanks for the tour."

"My pleasure." Melanie's saleswoman persona was back, and she gave them a little wave as she slid in behind the wheel and drove away.

"Wow, I had no idea that place was so run-down," Jazz

said as they walked back to her grandparents' place. "They'd be lucky to sell even if my B and B wasn't up and running."

"I don't know," Dalton said, his expression thoughtful. "She's right about the potential. The property location is incredible, and with a little work and a new design, the place could be stunning."

She glanced at him in surprise. "You really think it's a property worth flipping?"

Dalton shrugged. "Maybe. How's the market in this area?"

"Better than average." Jazz glanced back over her shoulder at the Stevenson place. "We had a lot of offers on our grandparents' house despite the depressed economy."

All her cash reserves had been pumped into the B&B, which was unfortunate because the idea of flipping a house with Dalton was extremely appealing.

On many levels.

Too bad, it wasn't meant to be.

"Pizza okay for dinner?" Jazz asked. "It's too late to cook."

"Works for me," he agreed. He didn't really care what they ate for dinner. He couldn't seem to get the Stevenson property out of his mind.

He'd noticed how Jazz's expression had lit up with the thought of flipping the place. As Melanie had toured them around, he'd been redesigning the entire interior in his head.

It was an excitement he hadn't felt in too many months to count. Quitting his job had been the right decision, there was no way he was ever going back to that rat race. But Jazz's comments about what Debbie would say about his choice of being a drifter had hit home.

Because deep down he knew his wife would be furious about how he'd abandoned his talent. If she'd forgiven him for the role he'd played in their deaths, that is.

He'd started drawing buildings at a very young age, encouraged by his father who'd also been an architect. Even as a kid, he'd found buildings fascinating. Old ones, new ones, half-way demolished ones . . . they'd all held a certain appeal.

His fingers itched to draw again.

"Dalton?" Jazz waved a hand in his face, distracting him from his thoughts. "Care to share?"

"Huh? Oh, nothing. I was just thinking about the Stevenson house."

She set the steaming hot pizza on the table between them. "She never told us what they're asking for the place. Guess she was too embarrassed to say after the way we pointed out the various flaws."

"Yeah, and based on her reaction, it's clearly overpriced." Dalton took a bite of pizza, watching as large raindrops splattered against the window. "There's a storm rolling in."

"Good thing the gazebo is finished," Jazz said, popping a slice of pepperoni into her mouth. "From here on, it's all inside work."

He nodded, chewing thoughtfully. Just how much was the Stevenson property listed for? And how much would the brothers be willing to negotiate on their asking price?

A fair amount, he guessed. Between the rotten bathroom floor and the B&B next door, they would be lucky to unload the place at all.

If not for the lakefront location, that is.

He thought about the bank accounts he'd walked away

from almost a year ago. He'd sold the house he'd shared with Debbie and put that money into a separate bank account. At the time, the amount had been substantial, and since he hadn't touched a dollar of that money it should still be there plus a little extra interest.

When he'd decided to leave town with only his knapsack on his back, he'd also challenged himself to live off of whatever cash he'd earned along the way. It hadn't been too difficult, he'd done all sorts of odd jobs, from washing dishes to being on a roadside crew. Handyman work was the most rewarding.

There had to be enough money in his bank accounts to buy the Stevenson house outright. Although he'd still need extra cash for the renovations.

More than doable if the bank would agree to a home equity loan.

"Did you check out my paint job in the blue room?" Jazz asked.

"Not yet." A loud rumble of thunder had him glancing up at the ceiling. "I hope your roof is in good shape."

"It is, my granddad had it replaced a year before he died." Jazz's smile faded. "The attic is full of the things they left behind after they passed away. Of course, their best pieces are here, especially in the great room, but I bet there are more hidden gems. Once all the renovations are finished, I want to go up and look through everything. Hopefully, I can find some additional furnishings to use in the guest rooms."

"Antiques are amazing," Dalton said with enthusiasm. "I'd be happy to help repair anything that's broken."

She tipped her head to the side, eyeing him curiously. "Really? Will you be here that long?"

He opened his mouth to answer, then closed it again

without speaking. It was a good question. One that he'd had no trouble answering until now.

The silence grew uncomfortably long.

"Never mind," Jazz finally said. "I didn't mean to push. Obviously, it's a decision you need to make when you're ready." She downed the last bit of pizza, then rose to her feet. "I'll take care of the dishes."

"I can help," he protested.

She shook her head. "I could use some time alone, if you don't mind. Although the way it's pouring outside, you might want to consider spending the night in the master suite. You'll be drenched by the time you get into your tent."

Staring out at the pelting rain, he silently admitted she had a point. Why bother sleeping in cold and wet conditions when there was a perfectly good bed inside?

Yeah, no doubt about it, he was getting soft.

He'd already showered and washed the clothes that were full of plaster dust. Conscious of Jazz's request for some alone time, he went into the living room area to the bookshelves lining each side of the fireplace. There was both fiction and non-fiction, so he chose a murder mystery and returned to his room to read.

The storm raged overhead, lightning flashing across the sky followed by the rumble of thunder. Several lightning strikes were loud enough to make him jump.

He set the book aside and padded back out to the French doors overlooking the lake. A crack of lightning hit close, rattling the windows.

"Dalton? Did you hear that?" Jazz rushed downstairs, visibly shaken. "It sounded way too close."

"Yeah." Dalton moved to the side kitchen window that faced the Stevenson's place. Was it his imagination or was there smoke coming from the corner of the roof closest to them?

He pressed closer, peering through the rainy darkness. Lightning flashed across the sky providing enough light for him to clearly see a streak of charred blackness extending from the roof all the way down to the base of the home.

The Stevenson house had been struck by lightning!

12

"Where's your phone?" Dalton asked, his eyes wide with alarm. "You need to call nine one one about a possible fire at the Stevenson house from a lightning strike."

Jazz pulled her mobile phone out of her pocket and did as he asked, her heart thumping wildly in her chest. Good heavens, what if lightning struck here?

"Wait! Where are you going?" She followed as he headed toward the French doors.

"Out to make sure there isn't a fire burning inside the place." He ran right out into the pelting rain.

She paced, waiting for the dispatcher to answer. A female voice finally came on the line asking what her emergency was.

"The Stevenson house has been hit by lightning."

"Is anyone hurt?"

"No, the house is for sale, and I don't think anyone is living there."

"I'll let the volunteer fire department know," the dispatcher said, then disconnected from the line.

Jazz tucked the phone away and cupped her hands against the glass so she could see out the window. She hated feeling helpless and had no idea what Dalton thought he was going to be able to do in the pouring rain. Why would he think there was a fire inside the house when the strike had been on the outside?

Maybe an electrical fire? She'd heard of fires starting inside the walls, moving along the electrical wires from outlet to outlet. The image made her grimace. Not good. Even though she suspected the Stevenson brothers might be the ones responsible for her vandalism, she wouldn't want to see anyone lose a house due to a fire.

A flash of lightning brightened the sky, but she couldn't see anything but the black charred ridge running down along the side of the house. She'd lost sight of Dalton. Had he gone around to the other side of the property?

Time ticked by slowly with still no sign of Dalton or the volunteer fire department. How long would it take them to respond? A little disconcerting to realize that if anything happened here at the B&B, the old house would be at the mercy of volunteers.

Just as she was about to head outside to search for Dalton herself, the French doors rattled and Dalton stepped inside, water rolled off him and pooled at his feet, as if he were a human fountain.

"Stay there, I'll get towels." Jazz hurried into the master suite that ironically smelled like him and grabbed two towels from the bathroom closet. In the main living area, she tossed them at Dalton.

"Sorry about the mess," he said. "The good news is that I don't think there's a fire simmering inside the house."

"And what were you going to do if there was?" she asked, feeling exasperated.

"Break a window to get in, then attempt to put it out," he responded. "The fire department hasn't even arrived. The place would be a total loss if I didn't do something."

"It's not our house to save," she reminded him. The wail of sirens growing louder was reassuring. Help would soon arrive. "The fire truck is on their way. Besides, I'm not even sure the Stevenson brothers would appreciate your efforts on their behalf."

"Maybe not, but it's a moot point regardless." He wiped the towel over his head, then wrapped it around his soaking wet clothes. He toed off his construction boots and left them to air dry. "I'm, uh, going to need to put everything I'm wearing in the laundry for the second time today."

"You think?" She couldn't help but smile. "It's not a problem, throw the towels in, too."

He nodded, then disappeared down the hall leaving a trail of wetness behind.

Unfortunately, she didn't have any spare clothes that would fit him. A sweatshirt, maybe, but no jeans or male sweatpants. She'd noticed that he only had two different sets of clothes to wear and figured that was all he could carry in his knapsack.

If only he'd consider sticking around for a while . . .

No, not just a while.

Forever.

Her heart squeezed in her chest because she was already way far down the path to heartache. Yet knowing that, she still couldn't find a way to turn back. Worse? She didn't even want to.

She was falling in love with Dalton. His kisses were addicting, and she enjoyed being with him. Far more than she'd ever liked hanging out with Tom.

Deep down, she sensed that Dalton wanted to stay, too,

but was stubbornly refusing to give in to the idea of moving on with his life without his wife and son.

What had caused their deaths? The unknown answer plagued her, although logically she knew it didn't matter. Whatever Dalton had done was in the past.

He was a different man now. A sweet, kind, generous man. One who deserved a second chance.

And so did she.

She watched through the window as the firefighters circled the house, checking things out. They broke open the front door and disappeared inside.

"What's going on?" Dalton asked. He was wearing clean dry clothes, but his dark hair was still plastered against his head.

"They just broke in," she told him. "I'm sure the Stevenson brothers won't be happy."

"Nothing they can do about it," Dalton said. "Why don't you head back up to bed? I'll keep an eye on things down here."

Jazz nodded, rubbing her hands up and down her arms, chilled despite the warmth inside the house. Before she could head upstairs, there was a loud knock at the front door.

She glanced questioningly at Dalton, then went over to see who was there. It was the female deputy from almost a week ago.

"Deputy Waldorf," Jazz greeted her. "Come in."

"Thanks." The woman wasn't as soaked as Dalton had been. "I have a few questions about what you saw this evening."

Jazz gestured for Dalton to join her. "Dalton was the one who saw the lightning strike, I only heard it."

Deputy Waldorf turned toward Dalton. "You actually saw the lightning strike the house?"

He looked a bit taken aback. "Not exactly, was looking out at the lake when I saw the flash and heard the strike. That's when I noticed the seared streak running from the roof to the bottom of the house."

"And where was Ms. McNally when that happened?" she asked.

"I was upstairs in my room. I came running down when I heard the strike. It was so close, I feared my house had been hit."

"Hmm." Deputy Waldorf made a few notes with a stubby pencil in a small notebook.

Jazz didn't appreciate the woman's tone. "I'm getting the sense you think I'm the one who did something to the house."

Deputy Waldorf shrugged. "I need to investigate. After all, you made it quite clear you feel the owners of the house next door are the ones committing vandalism against your property. Maybe you decided to get even with them."

"That's ridiculous," Dalton snapped, stepping protectively in front of Jazz. "How would she cause that sort of damage? It's clearly the result of a lightning strike, and I resent you implying otherwise."

Jazz put a hand on Dalton's arm. "It's okay, Dalton."

"No, it's not okay." The muscles in his forearm were tense. "Bad enough that old man Tate is holding some old grudge against you, but to listen as the police drag your name through the mud is unforgivable."

"Calm down, Mr. O'Brien." Deputy Waldorf shut her notebook and tucked it away. "This is all part of our routine investigation. I'm here to validate the facts, nothing more."

Jazz couldn't believe how Dalton had rushed to her

defense. It was sweet, but unnecessary. She sent an apologetic glance at the deputy. "I understand you have a job to do."

She nodded. "Thanks for your cooperation." Then she frowned. "What was that about Leon Tate holding a grudge against you?"

"He's a crabby old man, told me to get out of town." Jazz waved it aside. "I'm sure it's nothing to worry about."

Deputy Waldorf made another note. "Doesn't hurt to check it out. Well, thanks again for your cooperation."

"Any time." Jazz opened the door for the deputy, closing it and locking it behind her. She smiled at Dalton. "Thanks for being my knight in shining armor."

He looked embarrassed. "It's crazy that she insinuated you would intentionally damage someone else's property. It's one thing to get the facts, it's another to basically accuse someone of malicious intent."

She wanted very badly to hug him and kiss him but held back. "Well, good night."

"Good night, Jazz."

Walking away from Dalton wasn't easy, she could feel his gaze burning into her back as she ascended the staircase to the second floor.

At the top, she paused and sneaked a glance over her shoulder, expecting to see Dalton still standing there.

But he wasn't.

Apparently, she'd imagined his gaze on her. Maybe the camaraderie she felt was only in her head, too. She went into her bedroom, feeling sick at the knowledge that the feelings she had for Dalton were likely one-sided.

And likely to stay that way.

DALTON FORCED himself to walk away from Jazz, lest she figure out how deeply he'd come to care about her.

Looking back, he realized his reaction to the Deputy's questions were a bit over the top. The woman hadn't outright accused Jazz of anything, but he'd jumped all over her regardless.

The very thought of anyone hurting Jazz brought out every protective instinct he possessed.

He tossed and turned during the night; his gut twisted into knots as he wrestled with feelings he didn't understand.

The following morning, he rolled out of bed at the crack of dawn, driven by a sense of urgency. He needed to get started on sanding the bathroom grout in the blue room so he could get to work on the actual tiling.

He was surprised to find Jazz already in the kitchen nursing a cup of coffee. She looked as if she hadn't slept well either, and he wondered if the storm had kept her awake.

"Omelets for breakfast," he announced. "I'll cook."

Breakfast didn't take long, and soon they were back to their usual harmony as they planned the renovation strategy. Jazz would sand the walls in the blue bathroom while he began tiling the yellow room. That way she could add another coat of paint in the afternoon, after the dust was taken care of.

The hours flew by quickly as they worked. Tiling was a tedious job that required significant attention to detail. More so in this case because he was doing the work for Jazz.

Scary how much he wanted to make her happy.

The day flew by, their break for lunch only long enough to eat a few sandwiches.

It took him the entire day to finish the tile in the yellow room. Jazz finished painting and came over to join him, staring in awe at how it turned out.

"Dalton, this is incredible!" She gently swiped her hand over the glistening tile. "It's perfect and looks like something out of a fashion magazine."

He was pleased by her reaction. "I'm glad you like it. I should be able to finish up the blue room bathroom tomorrow."

"The painting is finished in there already," she said. "Come and see."

He followed her across the hall to the blue room. The four-poster bed looked amazing against the navy-blue wall, and the rest of the room was clean and bright. He also liked the dark blue curtains she'd hung in there, along with the white bedspread dotted with tiny blue flowers.

"It's incredible," he said, impressed with her efforts. "You have a good eye for decorating."

"That's what comes from working in real estate," she admitted shyly. "But I think it turned out pretty good, too. Once the bathroom is finished, it will be ready to go."

"Tomorrow," he repeated.

"How do you feel about grilled ham and cheese with tomato soup?" she asked, stretching her head from side to side. "I'm not up to cooking a big meal."

"Fine with me." He reached up and gently massaged her slim shoulders. "But I'll make grilled ham and cheese while you heat up the soup."

"Deal," she said, groaning in appreciation as he worked the kinks out of her muscles. "Ohh, that feels amazing."

For him, too, but he kept his thoughts to himself. "Maybe you should treat yourself to a day at the spa once all the work is completed."

She glanced at him over her shoulder. "That seems a waste of money. A hot bath will do the trick." She stepped away, and he dropped his hands before he did something really crazy like kiss her again.

After they finished dinner, he caught a glimpse of movement at the Stevenson house. Through the window, he could see Melanie Ryerson and a short rather pudgy guy examining the charred portion of the house where the lightning had struck.

"Excuse me, I'll be back in a few minutes." He went out through the French doors and quickly strode over to join them.

Melanie's expression was strained. "Hi, Dalton. This is one of the owners of the property, Mr. Rich Stevenson."

Dalton shook Rich's hand, grimly realizing the guy couldn't possibly be the one he'd chased the night he'd slept outside behind the gazebo. He was too round, especially around the middle, not to mention shorter than the guy he'd chased by several inches.

"I'm sorry about your house," Dalton said, gesturing with one hand toward the damage. "The storm last night was really something."

Rich curled his lip. "I'm not so sure the storm caused this. I asked the police to do a full investigation just to be sure."

Dalton's temper began to simmer. Was this why Deputy Waldorf's questions had been so pointed? "What are you talking about? Look at it," he said in a sharp tone. "The burn goes from the roof to the ground. It wasn't made by a human hand, only a lightning strike causes something like that. I've seen it before, when lightning struck a tree near my house."

"So you say." Rich Stevenson didn't look convinced.

Melanie looked frazzled. "I spoke to the firefighters myself, and they agreed that the burn was caused by lightning. It's just one of those freak accidents of nature."

Dalton wondered why the guy was being so obtuse about the cause of the damage. It wasn't as if Jazz had anything to gain from trashing their house.

Just as he was about to ask about the price they were asking, a Sheriff's deputy vehicle rolled into Jazz's driveway. Deputy Lewis slid out from behind the wheel and walked over toward them.

"Mr. Stevenson? Thank you for agreeing to be fingerprinted today, and if you could please let us know when your brother will be in town, I'd appreciate it. The sooner we can check his, the sooner we can clear both of your names."

"I told you I had nothing to do with that petty vandalism," Rich said furiously. "It's insulting!"

"As I said, the sooner we can get your brother's fingerprints to rule him out as a suspect, the better," Deputy Lewis said in a calm tone.

"I'd think your brother would come in right away. Normally people are anxious to clear their names," Dalton pointed out.

Rich whirled to face him, his fingers clenched into fists. Dalton stood his ground, but of course, the older guy wasn't about to hit him in front of a deputy.

"Mark will be here soon," Rich said between clenched teeth. "Our mother passed away last month, and he's still trying to get everything squared away. One would think we'd be offered a little consideration, under the circumstances."

Dalton felt bad hearing about the loss of their mother. Maybe that's why they recently listed the property.

Was it possible they weren't responsible for vandalizing Jazz's home and gazebo?

But if not them, then who? The Tates?

"I'm sorry for your loss," he said, meaning it. "I know it's not easy to lose someone you care about."

Rich looked mollified. "No, it isn't."

"Well, don't forget to send Mr. Mark Stevenson my way," Deputy Lewis said. "Take care now."

The deputy left as quickly as he'd arrived. Dalton wondered if he'd mentioned clearing Rich's fingerprints to Jazz or not. It didn't mean much yet, not until they had Mark's prints on file.

Dalton turned to head back toward Jazz's house, then paused and glanced back at Melanie. "What's the asking price on this property?"

Rich and Melanie exchanged a long look, and Dalton could tell that Melanie had urged Rich to lower the price from his original asking price.

She named a sum that was still too high but closer to what he estimated the value to be.

"Are you interested in buying?" Rich asked, his expression hopeful. The guy's previous rudeness had vanished. "It's a great place, you won't find a better location this close to the lake."

"Maybe," Dalton said. "But I think that price is still too high, especially considering this most recent damage."

"We're willing to entertain any reasonable offer," Melanie interjected with a bright smile.

Dalton stared at her for a long moment. "Good to know. I'll be in touch."

As he headed back to Jazz's house, he could hardly contain his excitement. He was going to place an offer, and by the looks of things, the Stevenson brothers would likely accept.

He was putting down roots in McNally Bay.

13

When Jazz saw a much older version of Rich Stevenson than she remembered as a child, she bolted out of the house and headed over to join them. It was encouraging that Deputy Lewis was involved in the conversation, but by the time she arrived, she only heard something about fingerprints.

"What happened?" she asked, as she and Dalton returned to her house.

He explained that Rich's fingerprints weren't a match to the prints found on the sledgehammer, but they were waiting for Mark to come in to test his.

She thought it was interesting. If the brothers were working together, Rich could have done the website destruction, leaving the physical stuff to his brother. And the fact that Mark hadn't shown up yet to cooperate with getting his fingerprints tested made her wonder if he was trying to hide his guilt.

Dalton disappeared into the master suite, and she didn't see him again until the next morning. He was already hard at work tiling the blue room. She squinted at the clock, unnerved to see it was barely past 6:00 a.m. Was he trying to finish up the last of the tile work before he left town for good?

She left him to it, heading downstairs to start breakfast. As she made French toast, finishing up the last of the bread, she tried to think of a way to convince him to stay.

Sticking around had to be his decision, but surely there was something she could say to help change his mind.

Unfortunately, no bright ideas were forthcoming.

She walked over to the staircase leading up to the second floor. "Breakfast is ready."

"Be down in a minute."

Jazz sipped her coffee as she waited for Dalton to come downstairs. He looked happy and well rested, different from the way he'd seemed yesterday.

Not that she should talk, she'd been rough around the edges yesterday, too. Even today, she couldn't shake off the impending sense of doom.

"This is great, thanks." Dalton dug into his breakfast with enthusiasm. He looked happy, fit and full of life, and she wished he could see how much he'd changed since they first met, when he'd asked for work.

Was it really only nine days ago?

She went still, wondering how it was possible for her life to change so dramatically in such a short period of time. Of course, the same thing had happened the night of her rehearsal dinner, but in the here and now, that seemed like a lifetime ago.

She didn't care about Tom or Megan, for that matter. Somehow, things had worked out exactly the way they were meant to. Starting a new business with her twin sister was exciting, and despite the odd Tate family feud toward the McNallys, she liked the small-town life.

"I, um, have to head into town early this afternoon," Dalton said. "Do you mind giving me a ride? Is there anything else you need from the hardware store?"

She wanted to ask what sort of errand he needed to attend to but managed to keep her insatiable curiosity in check. "Actually, I do need groceries, so we can go whatever time works best for you."

"Great. I'd like to finish the tiling first, though. I was able to get an early start, so I should be finished by one p.m. or so."

"Do you want to have lunch in the diner?" she asked. "Or we can try somewhere else, if you'd rather avoid the Tates."

"Oh, I don't think the Tates are a threat after the way you handled them last time." Dalton grinned. "In fact, I hope they are there again, we can kill them with more kindness."

She chuckled. "Yes, that was pretty amazing, wasn't it? I think that's only the second time I rendered someone speechless."

"What was the first?"

Her smile faded. "When I caught Tom kissing Megan, and I mean really kissing her, as if they were in need of a private room somewhere. I told him the wedding was off but that I'd be happy to donate my wedding dress to Megan if they still wanted to make good use of the church and reception hall."

His eyes widened. "You didn't."

"Yep, I sure did." She shrugged. "Then I tossed his ring at him. I was pretty civil, considering. I think most women in that situation might have thrown a bridezilla hissy fit. But I kept my cool." The night had once been imprinted vividly in her mind, but now it was a foggy memory.

"Pretty impressive."

"Yeah, but now that I think about it, that should have

been my first clue that I didn't love him the way I should love the man I was planning to spend the rest of my life with. I was more embarrassed about telling my family, particularly my four older brothers, that the wedding was off than losing Tom to another woman."

Dalton surprised her by reaching across the table to take her hand. "You're better off without him."

"I know." She dropped her gaze to their joined hands for a moment, wishing for more, before coming to her senses and pulling away. "I'm happier here, fixing up my grandparents' home so I can run my own business, than I would have been staying in Bloomington with Tom."

Dalton looked thoughtful for a moment. "Yeah, I have to agree this is a nice area. I've never spent a lot of time on the water, and I have to say it's really incredible being on the lakefront like this."

"A nice place to put down some roots," she said suggestively. "A place to start over."

Dalton nodded in agreement but didn't say anything more. Instead, he finished his French toast and downed the last of his coffee. "I hate to leave you with the dishes again, but . . ."

She waved him off. "Go, it's no problem. I can't do the tile work the way you can."

"Thanks." Dalton flashed a grin and disappeared back upstairs to the blue room.

There was something different about Dalton, but she couldn't quite put her finger on what exactly it was. He hadn't jumped on her comment about McNally Bay being a great place to put down roots, so it couldn't be that he'd had some sort of abrupt epiphany.

And what in the world did he need to go into town for

anyway? She couldn't imagine what errand could be so important.

She washed the breakfast dishes, then wrote up a grocery list. Although much of what she needed to buy depended on whether or not Dalton was staying or going.

Deciding to hope for the best, she increased the quantities of food to include him. If he didn't stay, she'd make the meals anyway and freeze the leftovers for when Jemma and Trey arrived.

She spent a couple of hours online, drafting a wedding package that would offer the gazebo and the entire B&B for one low price. Of course, that required a bit of number crunching, and math made her head hurt.

But she was able to figure it out and smiled with satisfaction at the possibility of hosting weddings there. Then she counted up the extra bookings she'd gained by opening the B&B sooner. In a matter of days, she'd doubled their reservations. There were still lots of open dates, though, especially for mid to late summer, but hopefully their little business would keep growing.

Offering the wedding package would help. She took an extra hour to figure out the best places to advertise her wedding package and picked a few free sites, along with a couple of paid ones.

You had to spend money to make it, right?

When she'd finished updating her website, she put the laptop computer aside and went to work on some basic chores she'd neglected over the past week.

Just before one in the afternoon, Dalton came looking for her. "Come check out the bathroom and let me know what you think."

She followed him upstairs and into the blue room. When she caught a glimpse of the bathroom she sucked in a quick breath. "Dalton! It's incredible! Look at how the tile sparkles in the light!"

He beamed with pride. "You were the one who picked it out, and it works perfectly in here."

"I absolutely love it." She smiled up at him. "I think the blue room is now my favorite one of all. I'm going to use this as the bridal suite, if anyone signs up for my wedding package, that is."

"They will," Dalton said with confidence. "It's an awesome marketing plan."

She wanted to hug him but held back, unsure of their relationship. Were they back to being friends? Their last kiss was fresh in her mind, but he hadn't made any further attempts to kiss her again.

It was depressing to think he didn't want to.

"So, ready to hit the town?" Dalton asked. "I'll need a few minutes to clean up, but then I would like to get going."

"Sounds like you're in a bit of a rush."

He nodded but didn't elaborate.

Ten minutes later, Dalton joined her in the truck. As she drove into town, she glanced at him. "Lunch first? Or errand?"

"Drop me off at the bank first" he suggested. "This shouldn't take too long, and I can meet you at Daisy's."

Bank? What did he want at the bank? "Oh, that reminds me, I need to pay you for the past couple of days."

"Not now," Dalton said. "We can talk about that later."

"Okay." She could barely contain her curiosity. She braked to a stop near the bank entrance. "Meet you at Daisy's."

Dalton slid out of the passenger seat and strode purposefully into the bank. She sat in the parking lot for a long minute until someone beeped their horn at her, demanding she move out of the way.

Jazz headed over to Daisy's and snagged the last open booth overlooking the street. Then she glanced around the café, looking for Leon Tate or his daughter, Mary.

They weren't dining today, or maybe they'd been and gone. Their animosity was still puzzling, but she chalked it up to nothing more sinister than simple jealously. Relaxing, she ordered a lemonade and sat back to wait patiently for Dalton to finish whatever he was doing at the bank.

After fifteen minutes, she grew fidgety. Her stomach was growling loud enough to be overheard by the other patrons, so when Ashley approached her for the third time, she broke down and ordered a cheeseburger, loaded with the works.

Halfway through her burger, she began to worry. Maybe Dalton's errand wasn't going very well. Was he looking into a loan to buy a car so he wouldn't have to hitchhike any longer? Or maybe he needed a loan to get money to pay for a cheap place to rent here in the McNally Bay area.

She hoped it was the latter.

Could she and Jemma afford to provide Dalton a room of his own for a while? Maybe, if he agreed to start working on the garage apartment. It might be worth the loss of revenue to gain the additional living space.

Yet, she already had reservations for all their available rooms rolling in. This was something she'd have to discuss with her twin as it would impact both of them.

She glanced at her watch again. Where was he? Then she saw him, jogging toward the diner. When he caught sight of her through the window, he waved.

Thank goodness, she thought, waving back. He pulled open the door and came over to join her.

"That looks good," he said, eyeing the leftover half of her cheeseburger.

"Ashley will be back in a moment I'm sure," she said.

"I have news," Dalton said just as her cell phone rang.

"Hold that thought." She pulled her phone out, frowning when she saw her sister's name on the screen. "Jemma? Is everything all right?"

"Hey, Sis, where are you?" Jemma's voice sounded strained. "Me and Trey are here at the B and B, a little earlier than planned."

"You are?" She glanced at Dalton. "And you're both okay?"

"We are now," Jemma said. "But I couldn't stay in Bloomington a day longer. Where are you? Am I interrupting something?"

"No, I was going to grocery shop, but I'll turn around and come home instead. Give me ten minutes, okay?"

"Okay, thanks."

Jazz disconnected from the call and threw Dalton an apologetic look. "I'm sorry, you'll have to eat my leftovers or order something to go. My sister is waiting at the house."

"Okay." He picked up her burger and finished it off in several quick bites as she flagged down Ashley for the bill. "I hope she isn't in trouble."

"Me, too."

Dalton had eaten the last of her French fries by the time Ashley brought their bill. She paid in cash, then hurried out to the truck, wondering what had happened to send her twin running to the B&B two weeks ahead of schedule.

Nothing good, that's for sure.

~

DALTON GLANCED at Jazz as she drove home, her foot firmly planted on the accelerator. Did she know that he'd placed an offer on the Stevenson place? At the time, he'd been excited by the possibilities. And about sticking around McNally Bay.

But now, suddenly, he was assailed by a wave of doubt. Maybe he should have talked it over with Jazz first. What if the renovation that needed to be done on the place didn't pay off in the end?

As Jazz pulled into the driveway, he saw a rusty green minivan sitting off to the side of the three-car garage. Obviously, it belonged to her sister.

Jazz threw the truck into park and slid out from behind the wheel at the same moment her twin came out to meet her. Dalton froze, seeing Jemma's blond hair and her young son, skipping toward Jazz, made his heart stumble in his chest.

Instantly, he flashed back to a time when Debbie and Davy had greeted him when he'd come home from work. Davy hadn't been walking, like Jazz's nephew was, but the grin he'd flashed at him had been nearly identical.

His knees went weak, and the magnitude of what he'd done hit him like a boulder falling off a mountain and landing on top of his head.

Jazz's twin sister and her young son were here to stay. A painful reminder of everything he'd lost.

"Auntie Jazz!" The boy clasped her around the waist, grinning up at her with his gap-toothed smile. "Mommy said you'd be here, but you weren't."

"I'm sorry, but I'm here now," Jazz said reassuringly.

Dalton edged away from the sweet reunion, moving into the house unnoticed. He went directly out the back to his tent and began breaking it down with practices movements, despite the way his hands were trembling.

He couldn't do it. He couldn't stay here after all. The reminder of how he'd lost his family was suddenly as acute as the night he'd been called by the police about the accident.

When he finished tucking the tent into his knapsack, he walked into the house, hoping to get his things from the master suite before Jazz noticed.

Too late.

"What are you doing?" she asked, her brow furrowed in confusion. "There's no need to leave, you can stay in one of the rooms upstairs for a while. Come on, I want to introduce you to my sister."

Dalton's expression was grim. "I'm sorry, Jazz, but I can't do this. I have to go."

The color drained from her face. "Go where?"

Anywhere, he thought. "Away." He brushed past her and quickly picked up his clothes from the bedroom, feeling desperate now about leaving as quickly as possible.

"Dalton, wait." Jazz reached out to snag his arm. The warmth of her fingers burned through his flannel shirt, searing his skin. He shook her off.

"What's wrong?" Jazz's voice was filled with tension. "Why are you suddenly so determined to leave town now? Is this related to something that happened at the bank? You mentioned you had news. I assumed it was good news, but if not, it's okay. We'll figure it out."

He'd forgotten about the stupid offer he'd put in. Well, it didn't matter, he could retract it with a simple phone call. He forced himself to meet her gaze. "This isn't related to the bank. Seeing your sister and her son . . ." He struggled with how to best put what he was feeling into words. "Seeing them brought back painful memories. I thought I could stay, but I can't. I'm sorry."

"That's ridiculous," Jazz said, her voice rising in anger. "Jemma and Trey are not your wife and son."

He narrowed his gaze, feeling his own temper begin to simmer. "You don't have a clue as to what I've gone through."

"No, I don't," Jazz agreed. "Because you haven't shared, other than you feel responsible for their deaths. But running away isn't the answer, Dalton. The only way you're going to survive is to figure out how to forgive yourself for your past mistakes."

"Forgive myself?" He knew his tone betrayed the depth of his self-contempt. And suddenly he couldn't stand it a second longer. "For putting my job before my family? For refusing to take off an extra day of work to accompany my wife and son on vacation? For forcing her to drive alone? She and Davy were killed that day when a semitruck jack-knifed on the freeway and struck their car head-on. An accident that wouldn't have happened if I hadn't made her wait until the end of the day before telling her to leave without me."

She winced in sympathy. "Dalton, I'm sorry, but—"

"No," he interrupted. The last thing he wanted was her pity. "There's nothing you can say to fix the past. Just like there was no excuse for my behavior that day." He swallowed hard and forced himself to continue. "I was the up-and-coming architect in the business getting all the big jobs and potential clients asking for me by name. I was making oodles of money but wanted more. My success went straight to my head. It cost me my family."

"I don't know what to say." Jazz's expression mirrored sympathy, something he didn't deserve. "Other than you've changed, Dalton. Maybe you didn't always make the best decisions back then, but you're a different man now. And you couldn't have known that a semitruck would cause a crash on the interstate."

She was missing the point. "I should have made my wife and my son the priority in my life," he repeated bluntly. Enough. He wasn't going to stand here and discuss it any further. His feelings weren't something he could turn off like a spigot. But when he turned toward the French doors, she jumped in front of him, as if she could physically prevent him from walking away.

"Please don't leave," she begged. "I care about you, Dalton. In fact, I'm falling in love with you. I was hoping you would agree to work on the apartment garage for us." She sent an imploring look. "For Jemma and Trey."

"I can't." If there was something he could do to change how he felt, he would. But there wasn't. Nothing would be the same in his life, ever again. "I care about you, too, Jazz. More than I ever anticipated. But staying here wouldn't be fair. You deserve someone who will love you with their whole heart and soul. And I can't be that guy."

Jazz looked devastated, and he almost crumbled beneath the pressure. With every ounce of willpower he possessed, he pushed past her and walked outside. He circled the gazebo, cut through to the Stevenson place, and headed out to the highway.

Never once looking back.

14

J azz didn't know how long she stood there, reeling from the ease in which Dalton had walked away from her.

It felt like hours but was likely only a few minutes.

"Hey, where's tall, dark, and gorgeous?" Jemma asked in a slightly forced tone as she entered the kitchen. "I thought you were going to introduce me to the handyman/architect who did wonders with renovating the place?"

Tears burned her eyes, and she attempted to subtly swipe them away. She cleared her throat. "He's gone. Apparently now that the work is done, he's decided to move on."

Her brave front must not have fooled her twin because Jemma rushed toward her, placing a consoling hand on her arm. "I'm sorry to hear that, Jazz. Are you okay?"

No, she wasn't okay. She'd been a fool to risk her heart on a drifter. But her issues weren't as important as what her twin was dealing with related to her ex-husband, so she squared her shoulders and forced a tight smile. "I will be," she assured Jemma.

"I'm here for you, Jazz," Jemma said.

"I know." Jazz gave her another hug, clinging to her sister like a buoy in a storm. "But it's my own fault, I should have known better than to fall for a drifter."

Jemma nodded. "I often wonder why you and I have been so unlucky in love when we grew up with parents that adored each other."

Jazz nodded. "Yeah, I know." She cleared her throat and released her twin. "Now, have you and Trey eaten lunch? If not, I'll run to the grocery store to pick up a few things."

"We stopped at Mr. Burger along the way." Jemma's expression was pained. "The food is atrocious, but Trey was thrilled with the special treat. It's the least I could do after what the poor kid has been through."

"Okay, then why don't you and Trey head upstairs to check out how everything turned out?" Jazz was desperate for a little time alone. "I need a few minutes to clean up the master suite for you and Trey."

"Sounds good." Jemma gently squeezed her arm before turning away. "I'll also start planning meals for the next few days. I need to make a list before we go to the grocery store."

Jazz nodded distractedly. She'd hoped the physical labor of cleaning the bathroom and laundering the bedsheets would help keep her emotions in check, but it didn't.

Everything in the master suite smelled like Dalton. Even after she finished cleaning.

Or maybe the scent lingered only in her mind.

Embarrassing really, to have confessed how she'd fallen in love with him. Obviously, he didn't feel the same way in return. Oh, sure, he admitted to caring about her, but that was a far cry from love.

How stupid was she? Why hadn't she realized that Dalton still loved his dead wife, considering how he tortured himself over causing her death and that of his young son?

Hearing the truth about what had happened only reinforced her opinion that he was a changed man. She'd assumed he'd caused their death by drinking and driving, but instead he'd sent them on a vacation without him and a semitruck had sideswiped them, killing them both outright.

It was tragic, sure, but hardly his fault.

But the craziest issue of all was that one look at Jemma and Trey had sent him running. What in the world was up with that? He must have seen other women with small children who may have reminded him of what he'd lost. Did he run from all of them?

She grimaced. Probably.

The urge to jump into her truck and follow him was so strong she twice headed to the front door, before catching herself.

Hadn't she told herself all along that Dalton needed to figure this out on his own? What was the point of chasing after him when he didn't want to stay?

When he didn't love her?

No, better to prioritize her time and energy toward the new business and to providing shelter and support to Jemma and Trey.

"Ready to head to the grocery store?" Jemma asked, waving a slip of paper in the air. "I have the list."

"Sure. But there's no reason for both of us to go, why don't you stay here and get your things unpacked? Make yourself at home in the master suite."

Jemma tipped her head, regarding her thoughtfully. "Okay," she acquiesced. "I'll give you more time alone, but don't think you're going to mope around here for much longer than a day. He's not worth it. Any more than Tom was worth it."

She instinctively opened her mouth to disagree, but then swallowed her protest. Truthfully, Dalton was twice the man Tom was. But it didn't matter because he didn't or couldn't return her feelings.

Maybe there was something unlovable about her. Tom hadn't loved her; Dalton didn't love her.

Enough with the self-pity party already! With renewed resolve, she snagged the list from Jemma and strode outside.

She didn't run across Mary Tate this time, and although a few people eyed her curiously, no one else tried to ram into her with a grocery cart. Jemma's list made it easy to get through the aisles in record time, and she headed home less than an hour later.

When she pulled into the driveway, she noticed another car sitting beside Jemma's minivan. When she saw the tall redhead, she realized it belonged to the real estate agent, what was her name? Oh yeah, Melanie Ryerson.

"Hello," Melanie greeted her warmly. "Do you know where Dalton is? I have exciting news for him."

News? Bank? The two clicked together. "He put in an offer on the Stevenson place?" It was a question, but she already knew the answer.

"Yes, and the brothers have accepted it." Melanie beamed with the thought of making money on the sale. "Isn't that exciting?"

She was still grappling with the idea that Dalton had actually decided to stay, up until they'd arrived home. Seeing her sister and her son had been the only reason he'd left? "Um, yeah, except for one small problem."

"Problem?" Melanie's smile slipped. "What do you mean?"

"He's gone."

"Gone?" Melanie stared at her blankly. "When will he be back?"

"He packed up his things and left." Jazz shrugged. "I don't think he's planning on returning."

Melanie's shoulders slumped in defeat. "Are you sure? Do you have a way to contact him?"

"Yes, I'm sure, and no, I don't have a way to contact him. As far as I know, he doesn't own a phone." Jazz opened the back of her truck and lifted out two bags of groceries. "I'm sorry."

"Me, too." Melanie looked as if she were about to cry. "If you do hear from Dalton, will you please let me know?"

"Sure," Jazz agreed, although she knew it was useless. Dalton wasn't coming back.

The rest of the day passed with painful slowness. Jazz did her best to push her heartache aside, but after Jemma and Trey disappeared into the master suite, Jazz found it impossible to stay inside.

She quietly eased out the French doors and stared blindly up at her beautiful gazebo for a long moment, barely noticing the cool breeze coming in from the lake.

Tears rolled silently down her cheeks, and she swiped them away impatiently.

She needed to get a grip. No one really died from a broken heart.

Well, except for her grandmother, who'd passed away within three months of Granddad. The difference being they'd been married for sixty-three years.

She'd only known Dalton for little more than a week.

Moving past the gazebo, she walked toward the lake, noticing how the serene it looked with the reflection of the moon glinting off the water.

She followed the lakeshore down to the Stevensons'. The house was dark, except for the single bulb emitting a weak light over the kitchen sink. Looking at the house, it was all too easy to imagine working with Dalton on the renovations inside, tackling the upstairs bathroom first, then moving down to the main level.

The image was so real, her heart squeezed painfully in her chest. Between the two of them, they'd easily turn the place into a showcase.

Just as she was about to turn away, a shadow moved at the corner of the house. A figure walked toward her. Dalton? Her heart leaped with anticipation only to crash when a familiar and unfriendly male voice said, "Hello, Jazzlyn."

"Tom?" She stared in confusion. "What are you doing here?" The moment the question left her mouth, she understood. "You?" Her voice rose with suppressed fear. "You're the one who's been causing the damage to my house? To the gazebo? To my website?"

He didn't respond, but the way he came closer had her taking a step backward.

Only she couldn't go very far because the lake was behind her. She considered making a dash for it, but Tom ran half-marathons for fun.

"Taking a sledgehammer to the gazebo is a little beneath you, don't you think?" She was desperate to stall for time. Maybe Jemma would realize she was gone and come looking for her. "And how did you figure out the password to my website?"

"You need to stop using the same one," he said with a smirk. Then his gaze turned serious. "Although it was smart of you to change the password to your bank account. That made me angry."

Good heavens, he'd attempted to clean out her bank

account? She stared in horror. "Why?" she said in a choked voice. "Why did you do this?"

"You ruined my life, Jazz," he said in an eerily calm voice. He took another step closer, and that's when she saw the thin wire stretched between his fingers. "It's only fair that I get to ruin yours."

She'd ruined his life? He had it all backward. Then again, apparently Tom only cared about himself.

She went still, considering her options. If Dalton were here . . . but he wasn't.

She was on her own, facing a murdering narcissist.

DALTON HAD ONLY GOTTEN as far as the Pine Cone Campsite when he realized he'd made a big mistake.

Jazz was right. There was no point in running from his problems. Not only that, but with every step he'd taken, her words had echoed in his mind.

I'm falling in love with you.

He didn't deserve her love. Just as he hadn't deserved Debbie's.

How was it possible that two women had loved him in one lifetime?

No, the better question was, how was it possible for him to fall in love with two women in one lifetime?

He loved Jazz. Had started to fall for her the moment she'd appeared in the doorway, holding a hammer, as if she wouldn't hesitate to use it, as she eyed him warily.

She was beautiful, warm, hardworking, down-to-earth, and fun. Everything he liked in a woman.

Even her stubborn streak and preference for old eighties music made him smile.

He'd turned his back on his old life but now realized that maybe turning away from the people who were important to him, like his parents, wasn't right.

Jazz's caring was a gift that he didn't deserve but longed to have anyway.

That's it. He spun around and headed back out to the highway. It had taken him five hours to walk here from Jazz's place and now he wanted to run back to her as quickly as possible. He stuck out his thumb, hoping he didn't have to spend another five hours heading back.

He forced himself to remember Jemma and Trey. So much like Debbie and Davy.

But he could admit now that the similarities were only in his mind's eye. Not in reality.

As he walked, holding his thumb out, he thought about what Jazz had asked. Would Debbie and Davy want him to spend the rest of his life alone?

Deep down, he knew the answer was a resounding no. Debbie didn't have a mean or nasty bone in her body.

A car slowed down beside him. He glanced over, surprised to see Melanie Ryerson behind the wheel. Her smile was hesitant. "Hi, Dalton. Need a ride?"

"That would be great." He took the knapsack off his shoulders and stored it in the back seat, before sliding in beside her.

"Where are you headed?"

He rubbed a hand over his jaw. "Back to the McNallys'." He hoped it wasn't too late.

"The Stevensons have accepted your offer," she said. "If you're still interested."

Surprisingly, he was. His heart quickened with excitement. "I am, yes."

"Great! Let's head back to my office to fill out the rest of the paperwork, if you have time that is?"

He wanted to get back to talk to Jazz, but maybe having the sale of the house squared away would work in his favor. He could show her not just with words but with actions that he was serious about staying.

"Why not?"

The entire ordeal took far longer than he'd anticipated. Afterward, he was relieved to know that within the next two weeks, since this was a cash deal, he could take ownership of the property.

And if he had his way, he'd start working on that upstairs bathroom first thing.

Melanie offered to drive him to Jazz's place, and he gratefully accepted. She dropped him off in the driveway, and he hesitated when the house looked completely dark.

Was it possible she was already asleep? It wasn't that late. He hadn't been hungry for dinner, but now he was ravenous.

Instead of knocking at the front door, he decided to head around to the back by the gazebo. If Jazz was asleep, he'd pitch his tent and wait until morning to talk to her.

"Don't come any closer." Jazz's voice was sharp with fear. "I mean it, Tom. Jemma will hear me scream and call the police."

"You'll be dead, and I'll be gone before they get here," a man's voice said.

Dalton silently set down his knapsack and dropped to one knee, digging around for his fishing knife, the only weapon he had. He desperately wished he had a phone, but the lack of one wasn't going to stop him from rushing to Jazz's defense.

He found the knife, then began to run directly toward

the man who was within arm's reach of Jazz. He held something stretched between his two fists, piano wire?

Was this guy really going to kill her?

"Hey, get away from her," Dalton shouted.

As he'd hoped, Tom spun around to face the new threat. Dalton was glad to have the guy's attention on him, hoping Jazz would take advantage of the diversion. She did, running away from Tom as fast as she could, hugging the shoreline.

Tom hesitated, then must have realized the odds were against him. He turned and ran in the opposite direction.

Dalton considered following him, but the guy was ridiculously fast and he'd already walked twenty miles that day, so he let him go.

"Jazz!" Dalton called out. "Are you okay? We need to call the police."

The sound of a car starting up proved Tom would be gone by the time the authorities arrived.

"Dalton?" Jazz altered her course to meet him. "What are you doing here?"

"I love you," he said. He tossed his knife to the ground and swept her into his arms, burying his face in her hair. "I'm sorry, Jazz. I was being stupid. Of course, your sister and her son aren't Debbie and Davy. I was just overcome with grief for a moment, scared to death to make another commitment. Will you please forgive me?"

"Yes, Dalton." She wrapped her arms around his neck and pulled him close, pressing a kiss to his cheek. "I forgive you."

He lifted his head and tried to read the expression in her eyes, impossible in the darkness. "I can't believe I almost lost you. I love you, Jazz," he repeated, in case she hadn't heard him the first time. "I didn't intend on falling in love ever again, until the day we met. Now I realize I can't live without you."

"Oh, Dalton, are you sure?" He could hear the wistfulness in her voice. "I don't want you to rush into anything. We have plenty of time."

"I'm sure," he said firmly. "The farther I went away, the more I realized what an idiot I was. Love isn't logical, it simply is. And I realized how fortunate I am to have found love not just once, but twice in one lifetime. You're a precious gift, Jazz, one I simply couldn't walk away from. I love you, and I bought the Stevenson place to prove I'm ready to put down roots here, with you." He paused, then added, "If you'll have me."

"Yes, Dalton," she whispered. "I'll have you, because I love you, too."

"Thank goodness," he muttered, then lowered his head to kiss her.

The kiss held the promise of a wonderful future. So much so that he didn't want to let her go. But eventually they needed to come up for air.

"Melanie will be thrilled you returned," Jazz said with a smile. "The Stevensons accepted your offer."

"I know. Melanie picked me up as I was hitchhiking back into town, so we finished all the paperwork. It's a cash sale, so we don't have to wait long."

"Really? It's a done deal?"

"Yes, the place is officially ours." He sobered, remembering the man who'd just threatened to kill her. "Come on, we need to go inside to call the police. Tom may have gotten away for now, but he can't hide forever."

Both Deputy Lewis and Deputy Waldorf arrived about fifteen minutes later. Jemma had come out to join them, and this time Dalton looked her straight in the eye and introduced himself.

"Glad to meet you," Jemma said. "But you should know if you hurt my twin again, I'll hunt you down and make you regret the day you were born."

Deputy Lewis cleared his throat. "Ma'am? It's not smart to threaten a man in front of a cop."

Jemma lifted a brow. "That wasn't a threat, Officer," she said, smiling sweetly. "It was a promise."

Dalton choked back a laugh. "Point taken," he said. "And I won't."

Jazz rolled her eyes and turned toward Deputy Lewis. "Here's what happened. I was walking along the lakefront when my ex-fiancé, Tom Duris, stepped out of the shadows at the Stevensons'. When I accused him of vandalism, he told me since I ruined his life, it was only fair he should ruin mine."

"That doesn't make any sense," Jemma protested. "He cheated on you, not the other way around."

"I believe he's a narcissist," Jazz said soberly. "He views the world and the people in it as existing only for his benefit. He wanted our real estate companies merged and decided the way to do that was to marry me. He told me his kissing Melanie shouldn't matter."

"The guy's a psychopath," Dalton muttered.

"Wait a minute, he actually confessed to the vandalism?" Deputy Lewis echoed in surprise.

"Not only that, but I heard him threaten to kill her," Dalton added. "He was holding a thin wire between his hands."

Jazz lifted her fingers to her neck, looking sick to her stomach. "I wanted to run away, but Tom's a marathon runner, so I kept trying to talk some sense into him. If

Dalton hadn't showed up when he did . . ." Her voice trailed off, and she shivered.

Deputy Lewis's expression turned grim. "Okay, try not to worry. We'll find him."

"You better," Dalton said in a low voice, wrapping an arm around Jazz. "Because he's evaded capture this far."

The two deputies exchanged a solemn look before Deputy Waldorf said, "If you can think of anywhere he might be, let us know."

Dalton did his best to hide his annoyance. "How many hotels and motels are there in the area? Have you started there? He's obviously been staying somewhere close by."

Deputy Lewis didn't appreciate his tone. "Yeah, in fact, we have been checking the motels in the area. And as I said, we'll find him, especially once we have his picture plastered around town."

Jazz put a hand on Dalton's arm, as if to settle him down. "Thanks, Deputy, we really do appreciate your efforts."

The deputies left, hopefully to do another sweep of the motels in the area. Jemma yawned. "Okay, kids, it's been a long day, so I'm heading to bed. Good night."

"Good night, Jem." Jazz gave her sister a quick hug.

When they were alone again, Dalton pulled Jazz in for another long kiss. When the room spun dizzily, he lifted his head and gently tucked a strand of her hair behind her ear. "I'm sorry I left you here, alone," he said in a low voice. "If anything had happened to you in my absence . . ."

"Shh, it's okay." She kissed him again. "We're both here now and that's what matters."

Dalton couldn't argue and tucked her head beneath his chin, holding her tightly.

Love was a precious gift. One that should never be thrown away. Maybe he'd made mistakes, everyone did.

But it's the choices you make after learning from those mistakes that really matter.

And this time, he vowed to do better with the second chance he'd been given.

Not just with Jazz, but mending the rift with his parents too.

Jazz wrapped her arms around his waist and leaned against him. "I love you, Dalton."

"I love you, too," he said.

In that moment, he knew that his ex-wife and son were both smiling down at him from heaven.

EPILOGUE

Six weeks later . . .

Jazz stretched upward in an attempt to ease the sore muscles in her back. Performing a complete overhaul of Dalton's new purchase was a much bigger job than renovating her grandparents' house had been.

But she loved the progress they were making. The bathroom upstairs was already completely redone and had turned out beautifully. The rotten subfloor had damaged the ceiling below and some of the walls, so when they went down to start that work, they'd decided to change the entire layout of the main level.

Dalton had created an amazing design, and Jazz just knew it was going to look incredible when they were finished. Yes, there was still a long way to go, especially because they needed to put up new support beams, but she didn't care.

It would all be worth the effort.

The only problem might be when it came to selling the place. She wasn't sure after all this hard work she'd be able to bring herself to let it go.

Not that it was hers to keep.

"Jazz?" Dalton called from the kitchen. "Do you want some lemonade?"

"Yes, please." She dropped the sledgehammer, the same one that had put the final nail in her case against her ex-fiancé. It had been no surprise that Tom's fingerprint had matched the one they'd lifted off the handle. With that evidence, along with Jazz's testimony, corroborated by Dalton as a witness, Tom had eventually been convicted of vandalism and attempted murder. He was still in jail, where he belonged, awaiting his sentencing hearing.

After that fateful night, it had taken Deputy Lewis a full week to find Tom, but they'd finally caught him going into a motel they'd already ruled out because he'd been using an assumed name. Apparently, the reason he was in debt was because he'd taken out huge cash advances on his credit card account. Using cash had enabled him to stay under the radar.

Jazz was just glad the entire ordeal was over. Especially since their B&B was seeing a nice, steady increase in business. She and Jemma were already making a modest profit, with more to come. Three brides had already scheduled weddings with them for later in the summer. Jazz and Jemma hoped that once the word got out they'd see even more reservations coming in.

And she'd even started talking to Megan again. Their friendship may never be as close as it had been, but when Megan found out what Tom had done, she'd been horrified.

And deep down, Jazz was grateful that Megan's actions had stopped her from marrying a narcissistic psychopath.

"Here." Dalton handed her a glass of icy cold lemonade. "Come on, let's take a walk."

She gulped from her glass, then followed him outside.

She'd been touched at how Dalton had invited his parents over to meet her. His mother, in particular, had given Jazz a hug, thanking her for healing Dalton's broken heart.

He took her hand and guided her toward the gazebo, which looked beautiful in the sunshine, the white structure accented with bright red geraniums hanging from each of the octagon-shaped corners.

The shade in the gazebo felt good. So far, they'd been having an unusually warm June. She hoped the weather would encourage more vacationers to come stay at the B&B. She drained her glass, and Dalton took it from her fingers and set it on the railing.

Then he took both of her hands in his, staring deeply into her eyes. "Jazzlyn McNally, do you have any idea how much I love you?"

She smiled, charmed by the seriously intent expression on his face. "Yes, Dalton, I do. Hopefully, it's just as much as I love you."

He stared at her for a long second, then slowly dropped down to one knee. He released one of her hands and reached into his pocket with the other. Her heart skittered sideways in her chest as she realized what was happening.

"Jazzlyn, will you do me the honor of becoming my wife?" He held out a modest but beautiful engagement ring. "Will you marry me and have a family with me? I promise to be a better husband and father this time around. I'll never let anything come before my family. You, and any children we are blessed with, will always come first in my life and in my heart."

She caught her breath as tears pricked at her eyes. She'd never experienced such a beautiful proposal. Too choked to speak, she held out her left hand, inviting him to slip the engagement ring on the fourth finger.

It fit, perfectly.

"Yes, Dalton," she finally managed. "Yes, I'd be honored to marry you and have a family with you."

He rose to his feet, swept her into his arms, and twirled her around in a circle.

"How did you know my ring size?" she asked, several minutes later.

"Jemma helped me," he confessed. "Good thing you both wear the same size."

"That sneak," she said, while making a mental note to thank her twin.

"Oh, and I don't want to sell the house," he added. "I'd rather live there with you."

Her smile bloomed. "I'm so glad because I don't want to sell it either. It will be perfect for our family."

Dalton kissed her soundly, then whispered, "This is the first day of the rest of my life."

She smiled through tears of joy. "For me, too, Dalton. I love you so much."

"Right back at you." He kissed her, and she knew that she wanted to marry Dalton right here, in the gazebo that helped bring them together almost two months ago.

The sooner, the better.

DEAR READER

Dear Reader,

I hope you enjoyed *To Love*, the first book in my new McNally Series. I love writing about families, and this idea came to me while I was vacationing in Ireland while staying in a B&B. I may be biased, but in my opinion, The McNallys' B&B is much better than the one I stayed in.

The next book in the series involves Jazz's twin sister, Jemma, and her son, Trey. I've included the first chapter here if you'd like to try a sample. This book is available for pre-order using this link. (insert link here)

Reviews are very important to authors, so if you would please consider leaving a review with the retailer you purchased this from, I'd greatly appreciate it. Also, please visit my website at www.laurascottbooks.com to sign up for my newsletter. I send them out to inform readers about my new book releases. As a newsletter subscriber you will receive a link to a free novella, *Starting Over*, which is part of my Crystal Lake Series. Lastly, you can find my author page here (insert facebook link) or on twitter @laurascottbooks.

Sincerely,

Laura Scott

PS Continue reading to see the first chapter of To Cherish

TO CHERISH

Chapter One

Jemma McNally kneaded a lump of dough while her three-year-old son, Trey, played with his miniature race cars in the living room. The lapping sound of waves hitting the rocky shore of Lake Michigan were audible through the French doors she'd opened to let in the balmy May breeze.

She put a little more muscle into the dough, determined to push her worrisome thoughts aside to focus on recreating her grandma's sourdough bread recipe from memory. She wanted to try it out before their first guests arrived the upcoming weekend. She and her twin sister, Jazzlyn, were holding the grand opening of The McNallys' B&B next Friday. Frankly, her stomach was knotted up at the thought of feeding a house full of strangers.

Cooking had always relaxed her, until now. The idea of turning her hobby into a business was intimidating to say the least.

"Daddy!"

Her son's voice sliced through her like a knife. Yanking

her hands from the dough, Jemma frantically raced into the living room, her gaze sweeping the area for any sign of Randal Cunningham, her abusive ex-husband.

"Trey?" Her gaze landed on the open French doors, and she immediately rushed outside.

Her three-year-old son was scurrying toward the gazebo on chubby legs. She caught a flash of something dark in the corner of her eye, but she didn't dare take her gaze off her son. Running as if her life depended on it, because it did, she caught up with her son, scooping the boy into her arms and clutching him tightly.

"Where?" Her voice was little more than a hoarse croak. Hunching her shoulders, bracing for a possible physical attack, she looked around the backyard. "Where's Daddy?"

"There." Trey pointed a stubby finger toward the lake. Off in the distance she could see a sailboat, but nothing else. She turned in a full circle, searching the entire area.

But there was nothing. No sign of the ex-husband she'd driven over a hundred miles from Bloomington, Illinois, to McNally Bay, Michigan, to escape.

A hundred and twenty miles and two state lines that didn't seem nearly far enough.

Feeling vulnerable out in the open, even late in the morning on a bright day, she whirled around and carried Trey inside the B&B, this time closing the French doors behind her. After setting Trey back on his feet, she made sure the doors were locked, willing her thundering heartbeat to return to normal.

There was no proof that Randal had been out there. She could have imagined seeing something out of the corner of her eye. And maybe Trey had mistaken the sailboat out on Lake Michigan for the old fishing boat her ex owned.

But fear gnawed at her. For a moment, she considered

calling her twin. Jazz was working with Dalton on renovating his recent home purchase located right next door. She pulled out her phone but then realized it was better to go straight to the police. She had a current restraining order against Randal, and if by some freak chance he'd actually enticed her son to go outside in an effort to kidnap him, she needed to notify the authorities.

At least she knew the Clark County Sheriff's Deputies weren't on a first-name basis with her ex, the way half the Bloomington Police Department was.

Ignoring the sticky bits of dough clinging to her trembling fingers, she made the call. The dispatchers voice was calm and soothing. "Clark County Sheriff's Department, what's the nature of your emergency?"

"I have reason to believe my ex-husband has violated the restraining order I have against him. I'd like to file a formal complaint."

"Are you safe?" the dispatcher asked.

Jemma grimly wondered if she'd ever feel safe, again. "I think so. I don't see anyone lurking outside. I'm at the McNallys' B and B."

"I'll send a deputy."

"Thank you." Jemma disconnected from the call, then made her way back into the kitchen to wash her hands and wipe down her phone. She placed a damp towel over the dough, then began to pace, wondering how long it would take the deputy to arrive.

She knew that Randal could find her here easily enough, considering McNally Bay had been named after her great-grandparents. She'd hoped and prayed that time and distance would work in her favor, but apparently not.

Silently ruing the day she'd met Randal Cunningham,

much less married him, she pivoted and paced the opposite direction.

"Look, Mommy!" Trey held up his chubby hand. "A police car!"

She forced herself to smile at her son, hoping he wasn't picking up on her distress. "It's great, sweetie. Do you have a fire truck, too?"

He nodded and searched his miniature cars until he found the fire truck. "Here, Mommy." He pushed it into her hand. "For you. Play wif me?"

"Sure." She dropped to the floor beside him, crossing her legs into the lotus position. She hadn't practiced any yoga since moving to McNally Bay, but maybe it was time to get back to it.

Heaven knew, she could use something to help her relax. This constant living in fear wasn't healthy.

For her or for Trey.

Ten minutes later, she heard the sound of a car engine. She stood and pulled a knife from the large butcher block, before cautiously approaching the front door.

Doubtful that Randal would be so stupid as to boldly approach the house, but she wasn't about to take any chances.

A brown sedan pulled to a stop in front of the B&B, the words Clark County Sheriff's Department stenciled along the side. Breathing out a sigh of relief, she quickly opened the door.

She inwardly groaned when Deputy Garth Lewis slid out from behind the wheel. Oh, he was nice enough, but he was also tall, with short dark hair and bright blue eyes, an impressive sight in his dark brown uniform. Far too attractive for his own good. This wasn't the first time she'd met him, he'd come to the house a few weeks ago when her sister had been almost killed by her ex-fiancé.

As a cop, he was the last man on the planet she'd be interested in. If she were open to entering into a relationship at all, which she wasn't. Bad enough that her one monumental mistake had nearly cost her everything she held dear, she wasn't going to even consider going down that path again.

Especially not with a cop.

"Deputy," she greeted him politely as he stepped into the great room. Next to the kitchen, she loved her grandparents' great room, with its cathedral ceiling, massive stone fireplace, lighthouse oil painting above the mantel, and the dark cherry antique furniture. She hadn't made it to the attic yet to find the silver candlesticks she was certain were packed away up there. "Thanks for coming."

"That's my job." He eyed the knife she still held in her hand warily. "What happened? The dispatcher said no one was hurt."

She flushed, feeling foolish for grabbing the knife. Turning on her heel, she headed back into the kitchen to put it away, then wiped the damp palms of her hands against her soft denim jeans.

"It's probably nothing—" she began, but was interrupted by her son.

"Policeman!" Trey's young voice held excitement, and she was upset to find her son approaching the deputy without an ounce of fear. "You're a policeman!"

Deputy Lewis grinned and dropped to one knee so he wasn't looming over her son. "I sure am. I see you have a police car in your hand there, too."

"Vroom." Trey waved the car around in the air. "Do you got one like this?"

"Not exactly. Mine is brown, matches my uniform, see?"

Trey nodded curiously, then reached out to touch his badge. "Mine," he said.

"No, it's not yours, honey," Jemma quickly came to her senses and crossed over to pull Trey's hand away from the deputy's badge. Despite what she'd gone through with Randal, it appeared Trey still idolized the police.

It wasn't his fault, she'd worked hard to make sure her son wasn't afraid of the authorities. Still, the possibility of Randal showing up in his uniform to secretly snatch Trey away haunted her.

Trey's lower lip trembled. "But I wanna badge . . ."

"How about this one?"

Jemma was surprised when Deputy Lewis pulled a shiny plastic badge out of his pocket. Her son's eyes lit up with delight.

"Thanks, policeman!"

Crisis averted for the moment, Jemma watched as Deputy Lewis clipped the toy badge to Trey's T-shirt. Her son began to strut around the living room with his chest thrust out. "I'm the police," he announced with glee.

"You sure are," Deputy Lewis agreed as he stood. He glanced at Jemma with a rueful smile. "Hope you don't mind."

"Of course not." Her voice sounded strained, even to her own ears. She tried to shake it off. "Would you like a cup of coffee?"

"That would be great, thanks."

She poured him a mug from the pot she'd recently brewed, her twin sister adored coffee while she preferred tea, and tried to get her rioting emotions under control. She didn't want to break down in front of the deputy, but the small act of kindness he'd shown her son had only highlighted the lack of a father figure in Trey's life.

All because she'd made the wrong choice in choosing Randal as a husband. Because she'd fallen for his lies. Because she hadn't escaped, sooner.

And now she lived in fear of losing Trey, forever.

Garth followed Jemma into the kitchen, the scent of yeast making his stomach rumble.

"Cream and sugar?" She glanced at him over her shoulder.

"Black is fine."

She handed him the mug, and he did his best to ignore the tingle of awareness he felt as her fingers brushed his. Idiot. He gave himself a mental head-slap. She was a woman in trouble, not a potential date.

"Thanks." He took a sip, eyeing her over the rim. She looked too young to have a son, with her deep brown eyes and blond hair pulled back into a ponytail. He knew she was Jazz's twin sister, but they were complete opposites. Jazz had dark hair and green eyes, compared to Jemma's blond hair and deep brown eyes. Jemma also had a streak of flour along her cheek, and he had to restrain himself from reaching up to wipe it away. He cleared his throat. "Why don't you take a seat and start at the beginning?"

Suddenly exhausted, she dropped into the closest chair. "It's probably nothing . . ."

"You brought a knife to the front door," he reminded her, wryly. That and the look of panic in her eyes had gotten to him in a big way. "It's not nothing. Go on."

She blew out a breath, a steely resolve in her gaze. "I have a restraining order against my ex-husband, Randal

Cunningham. He lives and works in Bloomington, Illinois, as a cop."

A cop? What were the odds? He winced. "I see."

"I was awarded sole custody because of a domestic dispute that turned violent." She dropped her gaze, as if unable to bear looking at him. "At the time, Randal didn't put up a fuss, no doubt because he wanted to keep his job. But that was nine months ago, and recently, he's made it clear he wants to go back to court to sue for joint custody of Trey."

Garth jotted down her ex-husband's name so he could pull up the court order. "What happened this morning?"

"I heard Trey call, 'Daddy,' and when I rushed in, he was outside walking toward the gazebo. I ran out to pick him up and asked him where he saw Daddy, and he pointed to the sailboat on the lake."

"A sailboat?" he echoed in confusion.

She nodded, staring down at her lap, where her fingers were twisted together. "My ex owns a fishing boat. I know Trey is only three and a half and could be confused about what he saw, but I want this incident on record, just in case Randal was here." She finally lifted her gaze to his. "I can't risk my ex-husband taking Trey away from me."

Garth understood her concern but also knew there wasn't much to work with. A three-and-a-half-year-old pointing at a sailboat on the lake and saying the word "Daddy" wasn't exactly a compelling argument that her ex had shown up here, violating the restraining order. "Have you noticed anything else?"

"I thought I saw something dark out of the corner of my eye, but when I picked up Trey and looked around, I didn't see anyone." Her gaze held dull resignation. "I told you it was probably nothing."

Yet that nothing had caused her to pick up a butcher knife before coming to the door. The idea of her ex-husband physically abusing her made him feel sick to his stomach. He'd been involved in several domestic incidents. In his opinion, they were the most dangerous call a cop could respond to. Emotions always ran high, and spouses or partners often acted out irrationally.

"Hey, it's a good thing to have this complaint on record," he said, even though he knew it wouldn't go anywhere. "When's the last time you've seen Randal?"

She shook her head. "Months. He used to call from a blocked number, so I had my cell number changed." She hesitated, then shrugged. "There was an incident at Trey's preschool a few weeks ago in April, where a man showed up claiming to be his father to pick him up for a doctor's appointment. Thankfully, the teacher said she had to verify with me first, so the guy left."

The close call made the back of his neck tingle. "Was she able to identify him as Cunningham?"

"No. She described a thin man with dirty-blond hair." Her tortured gaze locked on his. "Randal is big, built like a defensive lineman, not as much fat as muscle. He has black hair and used to have a black goatee. He may have shaved his face, but it still wouldn't change the rest of his appearance, much."

"That's odd," he muttered. "Unless Randal hired the guy?"

"That's what I suggested, but the police claimed there was no proof." Jemma sighed. "You need to know that a lot of the Bloomington cops believe the lies Randal tells them about me. They think I'm making all this up in an attempt to hurt Randal because of the divorce, as if he was the one who'd filed." There was a hint of bitterness in her tone.

"I'm sorry," he said, feeling helpless.

"Thanks, but it doesn't matter. That incident was the impetus I needed to send me packing up my stuff and making the move here to McNally Bay." Her attempt to smile was a bit pathetic, but he gave her points for trying.

Garth stared at the guy's name on his notepad realizing that it wouldn't be difficult to find Jemma McNally here at her grandparents' mansion. The whole town was named after them.

He didn't like thinking about her ex-husband showing up here, trying to get to his son. The boy was innocent in all this and was clearly a friendly kid.

One who didn't seem to be afraid of his father.

Was Cunningham right? Was Jemma stretching the truth to keep her son?

She didn't seem like the type to do that. And she had picked up a butcher knife. He scowled and tightened his grip on his stubby pencil, not liking the situation one bit.

"Please." Jemma's soft voice pulled him from his thoughts. "I need you to believe me. I need you to believe that Randal is capable of kidnapping his own son, and worse."

"I'll make the report," he said, not ready to admit whether or not he believed her. "I'll also ensure that all the deputies have a picture of your ex-husband in their vehicles. If he shows his face, we'll find him."

"Thank you." Jemma's tentative smile transformed her sweet features into stunning beauty. When she reached over to rest her hand on his arm, every muscle in his body went tense.

She quickly pulled her hand away, as if she'd surprised herself with the gesture. He hastily swallowed the last of his coffee and stood, anxious to get out of there. He couldn't afford to let his attraction for Jemma get in the way of doing his job.

That had happened once before with disastrous results. Kate's face and that of her four-year-old daughter, Sophie, flashed in his mind for a moment, before he ruthlessly shoved it away.

No way. Uh-uh. Wasn't happening.

He couldn't, wouldn't go down that painful path again.

Jemma and her adorable son were better off remaining distant acquaintances that he needed to protect.

He absolutely refused to open himself up to more heartache.

ALSO BY LAURA SCOTT

Healing Her Heart

A Soldier's Promise

Coming Home

Worth The Wait

Christmas Reunion

Second Chance

Made in the USA
Coppell, TX
29 November 2024